To:
Pa Pa Barr
From
Brittany, Jessie

MW00622270

# Vengeance is Mine

## Sequel to
## Death Rides a Pale Horse

Vengeance is Mine
Copyright © 2005
By Dusty Rhodes
All rights reserved.

Cover art: Holly Smith
Book Skins
Copyright 2005 ©
All rights reserved.

SUNDOWNERS
a division of
Treble Heart Books
1284 Overlook Dr.
Sierra Vista, AZ 85635-5512

Published and Printed in the U.S.A.

The characters and events in this book are fictional, and any resemblance to persons, whether living or dead, is strictly coincidental.

All rights reserved. No part of this book may be reproduced or transmitted in any form by any means, electronic or mechanical, including photocopying, recording, scanning to a computer disk, or by any informational storage and retrieval system, without express permission in writing from the publisher.

ISBN: 1-932695-09-5

## *Other Books by Dusty Rhodes*

Man Hunter

Shiloh

Jedidiah Boone

Death Rides a Pale Horse

Shooter

# Vengeance is Mine
## by
## Dusty Rhodes


Sundowners

A

Division of

Treble Heart Books

"Vengeance is mine, saith the Lord." (Rom. 12:19)

# Chapter I

The posse returned empty-handed. Tad Littlejohn and his friend, Lupe Raminez was hitching their team of Missouri Brown mules to the wagon when the straggling line of sweat-slick horses and riders rode slowly into town.

Members of the posse sat hunched in their saddles, completely spent from the long chase. Their hats were pulled low. A hot Texas wind tugged at their long dusters.

Steam billowed from the exhausted horses' nostrils and lather hung along their withers. Their heads hung low and each step was slow and labored. Sheriff Paxton spotted the two boys and reined his mount toward the livery.

For a long moment the lawman stared down at Tad Littlejohn before he spoke. Standing before him was the spitting image of the boy's father. The rough work pants, denim shirt, and suspenders couldn't hide the work-hardened boy inside. He was tall for a boy of fourteen, tall, wide shouldered, and narrow in the waist. His long black hair hung shoulder length. His high cheekbones and dark, flashing eyes told of his Indian heritage.

"I'm sorry, son," he said hoarsely through dry and cracked lips.

Tad didn't reply. It felt like a mule kicked him in the stomach. Inside his chest, his heart shattered into a thousand pieces. He swallowed a huge lump in his throat and blinked away tears that breeched his eyelids.

In that moment of time he realized that his life was changed completely—he would never be the same—he would never rest until his father's murder had been avenged.

The sheriff saw the change too. He saw the stony expression that washed over the boy's face. He saw the eyes narrow to thin slits. He saw the hard-set line of Tad Littlejohn's mouth and somehow knew the meaning.

The boy suddenly became a man. The expression in the young man's eyes was a terrible thing to behold. George saw the wide, fresh face of a fourteen year old, but the eyes of an infinitely older man. Sheriff George Paxton sadly dropped his head and reined his mount around to follow the rest of the posse down the street.

It had been two days since T. J. Littlejohn was gunned down in the street of Lubbock, Texas, shot in the back by the high and mighty rancher from New Mexico Territory, Buck Slade. The funeral was to be held that morning at ten, and then the body would be moved to the Littlejohn valley for burial.

The posse rode out within an hour after the shooting, but few, if any, really expected them to catch the killer. Slade was mounted on a superior horse and it wasn't that far to the edge of the Sheriff's jurisdiction.

Tad hardly said half-a-dozen words since the shooting. It wasn't that unusual for Tad. He was like his father, not much on talking. T.J. often said to him, "I don't recall ever learning anything when I was doing the talking."

Lupe was a different story. He talked about one thing or

another every waking minute. The two boys had become
inseparable since T.J. brought Lupe home from New Mexico to
live with them; they were like brothers.

The boys finished hitching the team and saddling their
horses. Tad slipped a lead rope on his father's buckskin and
tied him to the back of the wagon. They pulled the wagon with
their riding horses tied behind down the street to the hotel so
things would be ready to go after the funeral service.

Tad was worried about his mother. Mary hadn't left her
hotel room since right after the shooting. Tad's younger sister,
Marilyn, had carried her mother's food up to the room and seen
to her every need. His sister seemed to be taking her father's
death better than any of the rest of them, at least outwardly. She
was one who kept her feelings shuttered inside more than the
rest of the Littlejohn family. At twelve, she looked and acted
much older and he often thought of her as his older sister.

Sally was another matter. She remained quiet and moody
since her papa's death. She had been especially close to her
father. Rev. Hensley told Tad that the loss of a parent was
especially hard on someone only four years old.

Well, it was hard on someone fourteen years old too. But
he was older, *more man than most men,* his papa often said of
him, and he was supposed to understand death—then why didn't
he?

He didn't understand why papa got sick with whatever it
was that the doctors said was eating away his insides. He didn't
understand why that no-good back shooter killed his father. He
didn't understand any of it. All he understood was that Buck
Slade must to pay for what he did, no matter what, he had to
pay.

Tad and Lupe sat on the top step in front of the hotel, not
talking, just sitting there, both lost in their own thoughts.

"Looks like folks are starting to gather over at the church,"

Tad finally said. "Reckon we best get up to the room and put on our clothes for the funeral."

Pushing to their feet, they entered the hotel and climbed the stairs to the rooms that the sheriff arranged for the family to use.

Marilyn picked out funeral clothes for the whole family down at Mr. Stubblefield's store. She bought black broadcloth suits for both Tad and Lupe. She laid them out on the bed. Neither Tad nor Lupe ever owned a real suit before.

They both dressed in the unfamiliar-feeling clothes and went down to the lobby to wait for Mary and the girls. It hurt his heart when he saw his mother coming down the stairs. She was dressed in a solid black dress. Even through the thin black veil that covered her face he could see that her eyes were red and bloodshot from crying. Tad never saw his mother look so tired.

Both Marilyn and Sally wore dark blue dresses. Sally clung tightly to her older sister's hand as they walked side by side.

Sheriff Paxton was waiting outside on the boardwalk when they all walked out. He walked with the family to the church. The church house was packed. When they entered Rev. Hensley asked the audience to stand. The front bench was reserved for the Littlejohn family.

Tad only half listened as the audience sang *Amazing Grace*. After the song ended. Reverend Hensley stood and walked slowly to the pulpit. He opened his bible and began to read...

"The Lord is my shepherd, I shall not want. He maketh me to lie down in green pastures: he leadeth me beside the still waters. He restoreth my soul: he leadeth me in the paths of righteousness for his name's sake. Yea, though I walk through the valley of the shadow of death, I will fear no evil: for thou art with me; thy rod and thy staff they comfort me. Thou preparest a table before me in the presence of mine enemies: thou annointest my head with oil; my cup runneth over. Surely goodness and mercy shall follow me all the days of my life: and I shall dwell in the house of the Lord forever.

"Friends and neighbors, we come today on this sad occasion to pay our final respects to one of our own who has departed this life. T. J. Littlejohn was a good man, a devoted husband, a loving father, a helpful neighbor, and a good friend. He was one of us.

"I'm told that when T.J. first learned of his illness and that he had only a few months to live, his first concern wasn't for himself, but for his family. To my way of thinking, that's the mark of a great man.

"Though he is no longer with us in body, he will always be with us in spirit. His life touched each person in this room, and if, through the touching, your life has somehow been made better, then truly, T.J. Littlejohn's life was not lived in vain. His memory will live on in our hearts. Shall we pray?

"Our Heavenly Father, You have told us that you are the source of all comfort and that we ought to comfort one another even as we find comfort in you. We pray that you pour out a special helping of comfort on the Littlejohn family today, and in all the days to come. Amen."

"Now friends, please join together as we sing, *Beautiful Sunset.*

When the song ended Mr. Stubblefield walked to the front and opened the coffin. The people filed slowly by, paused and glanced down. Some of the women cried. Others said their farewells in their own way.

Finally the church was empty except for Rev. Hensley, George Paxton and the Littlejohn family, and one by one they escorted the family to the casket to say their final goodbye. With the help of the Reverend and the Sheriff, Mary and little Sally went first.

The girl-child nestled close against her mother's side and clung tightly to her mother's hand. The sadness and confusion in the small, soft face swelled the ache around Mary's heart. How could she explain T.J.'s death to her young daughter when she didn't understand it herself? What could she possibly say that would make the death of a father she loved so much, easier to understand for this little girl?

For long moments Mary stood there, staring into the coffin, struggling to compose herself. In a voice thick and grainy from crying and barely above a whisper, Mary spoke through choking sobs.

"I loved you like no woman ever loved a man, T. J. You were my strength, my life, my reason for living. I'll go on, but it will be a lonely journey without you. Rest now, my love, until we meet again."

She leaned forward and kissed the cheek of her departed husband and then turned slowly and led her young daughter back to their seat.

Marilyn was escorted next by the two men, one on either side. She stood quietly for a few moments, reached a hand and placed it over her father's heart, and then turned and walked slowly back to her seat.

Tad and Lupe sat side by side. Tad leaned forward in his seat with his elbows propped on his knees, his head was bowed and his eyes closed as if in prayer. He struggled hard to hold back the sobs that choked him.

Rev. Hensley and Gorge Paxton waited patiently. Finally, the two boys rose and walked forward. For several minutes Tad stood looking down at his father. His jaw set hard. His eyes narrowed. His fists clenched until his fingernails bit into the palms of his hands. One hand reached to rest softly upon his father's forehead, the other hand come to rest over his own heart.

When he spoke the words came out as chiseled and hard and cold as a tombstone.

"I love you, Pa. You taught me everything I know about life and living. If it's the last thing I ever do, I swear it on my life. I will make Buck Slade pay for what he done."

Sheriff George Paxton heard the boy's words and slanted a quick look, first at Tad, then at his mother. It was clear she heard her son's words too, for her face went white, her eyes widened and her hand flew to cover her mouth. There was little doubt she knew the meaning of her son's promise.

The journey from town to the Littlejohn valley was a slow and sad trip with little, if any, conversation. George Paxton drove the wagon carrying the coffin, his dappled gray horse tied to the back. Reverend Hensley sat in the seat beside the sheriff.

Tad drove their wagon, his mother sitting beside him. Marilyn and Sally rode in the floor behind the seat. Lupe, Jed Holly and Homer Green rode their saddle horses alongside the wagon carrying T.J.'s body. They volunteered to ride along to help with the grave digging and lowering the coffin.

Arriving in their valley late in the afternoon, the wagon carrying the coffin pulled to stop at the place Mary selected for the burial site, under the big oak tree on the hillside near the creek. It was her and T. J.'s favorite spot. The men immediately went to work digging the grave.

The family wagon proceeded to the house before stopping. Shep, Lupe's German shepherd dog, ran out to greet them. Tad and Marilyn helped their mother down from the wagon. He then took the wagon to the barn while the womenfolk went inside.

He untied his own saddle horse and his father's big buckskin and turned them into the corral. He poured some oats into the feeding trough, and then unhitched the team of mules and turned them loose to graze. After unloading the saddles and bridles from the wagon, he hung them from suspended ropes in the barn and then hung the harness from pegs along the wall.

He took a shovel from the barn and headed toward the creek to help the others with their task. With five of them working, the grave was soon finished.

Tad walked back to the house to escort his mother and sisters the quarter mile to the gravesite. The evening sun was dipping behind the western horizon beyond the pine-covered hillside. It was a long, silent walk.

The men threaded two long ropes underneath the coffin and stood with their hats in their hands as Mary and her children approached. Seeing Lupe standing with the men, she reached a hand, inviting him to stand with the family. He did.

Slowly, Mary lifted the large, well-worn family bible and opened it. She handed it to Reverend Hensley. With a loud, clear voice he read:

"For this we say unto you by the word of the Lord, that we which are alive and remain unto the coming of the Lord shall not precede them which are asleep. For the Lord himself shall descend with a shout, and with the voice of the archangel, and with the trump of God: and the dead in Christ shall rise first: Then we which are alive and remain shall be caught up together with them in the clouds, to meet the Lord in the air; and so shall we ever be with the Lord. Wherefore comfort one another with these words."

Mary took a step forward and laid a handful of wild flowers on the top of T.J.'s Casket, then turned and without a backward look, walked slowly back toward the house, sobbing, her face buried in the handkerchief in her hand.

# Chapter II

It was still dark when a soft, scraping sound jerked Tad awake. He flicked his eyes open and listened, and then relaxed as he heard soft footsteps moving around in the kitchen. *That would be ma building a fire to make breakfast*, he decided.

His father's admonition flashed in his memory, *"A man that ain't up and about before daylight never will amount to much, remember that, son."*

Tad swung his bare feet to the floor, stretched, and pushed upright. Lupe slept in the bed a few feet away and Tad shook him awake.

"Rise and shine, *amigo,* we've got a lot of work to do today."

Both boys pulled their work pants on, stomped into their boots, sleeved into their heavy denim shirts and pulled their suspenders over their shoulders.

Mary kept a fire going in the cook stove and water on for coffee when they walked into the kitchen.

"Morning, Ma."

"Morning, Mrs. Littlejohn," Lupe echoed.

Mary only nodded. Tad glanced at his mother. Her eyes were red and bloodshot. It was clear that she had been crying all night.

Lupe scooped up the water bucket off the wash stand and headed to the water barrel to fetch fresh water for breakfast. Tad took a seat at the long table and stared silently at the empty coffee mug before him.

As Lupe entered with the bucket of water, Tad looked up.

"After we milk and slop the hogs I expect we better see if we can round up our cattle and drive them back into the valley. Reckon they wandered off their grazing land while we were in town."

"I'll slop the hogs if you will milk old Bossy," Lupe said. "That ornery old cow just don't like me, she kicks me every time I try to milk her."

"You just got to know how to handle females," Tad laughed, punching Lupe in the ribs.

"And I suppose you are the *expert* on handling females," Marilyn said, walking into the kitchen and overhearing Tad's comment.

"Christine Holly thinks so," Tad told his sister.

"Is that right?" Marilyn shot back at him. "What did she say?"

"She said I seemed older than even the bigger boys at school, smarter too. She said that I knew how to treat a lady."

"How would she know? She wouldn't know a *lady* if she saw one. Besides, she flirts behind your back when you're not looking."

"Does not."

"Does too, I saw her making calf eyes at Rodney Sherman at Church the other day."

"*Rodney Sherman*! Chris wouldn't look sideways at—"

"That's enough!" Mary shouted, something she never did.

"Sorry, Mother," Marilyn said.

"Lupe, we best get at them chores if we plan to get them done before breakfast," Tad said.

The boys took the milk bucket and headed quickly out the door.

The eastern sky was giving birth to dawn. A dark gray tinged the horizon. The rooster crowed, welcoming the new day. Bossy bawled, voicing her displeasure at their tardiness as they approached the barn.

Always before, when T.J.'s big buckskin was in the corral, he trotted over to the gate when the boys approached and stuck his head over the fence wanting to be patted. This morning something was different. The gelding stood on the far side of the corral with his head over the top rail, staring toward the creek.

Deciding to go ahead and turn the buckskin out to graze, Tad lifted the rope loop and swung the gate open. Tossing his big head, the horse saw the gate open, wheeled, and charged out the gate in a burst of speed, its churning hooves sending dirt flying.

"What's wrong with Buck?" Tad asked his friend. "Where's he going in such an alfired hurry?"

The boys watched as the big horse galloped toward the creek, its mane and tail flying in the early morning light. The horse headed straight toward the gravesite where T. J. was buried.

"Would you look at that?" Tad said in amazement.

The buckskin stopped beside his master's fresh-dug grave. His big head lowered and sniffed at the mound of earth, his hoof pawed at the loose dirt.

"Ma!" Tad shouted, running as fast as his feet would carry him toward the house. "Ma, come quick!"

The door burst open just as Tad leaped onto the front porch.

"What is it?" His mother wanted to know. "What's wrong?"

"Look yonder, down by Pa's grave."

For a long minute Mary stared, her eyes shielded by a palmed hand.

"Seems we're not the only ones that will miss him," she said sadly, wiping her hands on her apron, she turned and went back to fixing breakfast.

The weeks dragged by slowly. Tad and Lupe worked from dawn to dark. Every morning the buckskin paid a visit to his master's grave, sometimes spending an hour or more, just standing there with his head bent low to the ground.

Winter was coming and there was no shortage of work to be done to prepare for its arrival. One day, while they were taking a breather from sawing the large logs into shorter pieces suitable for splitting, Lupe put words to a question that gnawed at him for weeks.

"Did you mean what you said at the funeral?"

Tad jerked a single nod, the way he had seen his pa do a thousand times. "What's the use of saying something if you ain't gonna do it?"

Lupe seemed to think about what his friend said and slowly nodded his head.

As the weeks passed Mary appeared to be snapping out of being sad all the time. She still suffered crying spells, but they seemed to be getting farther and farther apart. Lately, Tad even saw her smile from time to time.

The boys used the time over breakfast to lay out their work plans for the day.

"We need a load of feed from town," Tad said around a mouthful of biscuit and flour gravy. "Think I'll hitch up the wagon and take a run in today. You need anything from town, Ma?"

"We could use a sack of flour and a sack of sugar."

"Lupe, I'd feel better if you would hang around close while I'm gone."

"I'll split those logs we sawed up."

"Keep your rifle handy, just in case," Tad said.


The trip to town was uneventful. Tad liked his new adopted brother, but sometimes he just needed to be alone. Seemed like he could think better when he was by himself.

The sun was just shy of noon when Tad pulled his team of mules and wagon up to the back of Mr. Stubblefield's store. The storekeeper came out the back door wiping his hands on a dirty apron.

"Morning, Tad."

"Morning, Mr. Stubblefield. I'd like to pick up that stove Pa bought Ma if that would be okay?"

"Of course it is okay. I would have already brought it out but the time just got away from me. It's in the warehouse out back, just back the wagon up to the loading dock and I'll help you load it. It's all paid for and everything, your pa took care of that before..."

The storekeeper bit off his words.

"I need some feed too," Tad said. "I'd like to finish out the load with sacks of shorts for our hogs and a sack of corn. Ma needs a sack of sugar and a sack of flour too."

"How is your ma?"

"She's tolerable, I reckon. She sure misses Pa though. We all do."

"Terrible thing," the storekeeper said, "just terrible."

Tad backed the wagon up to the loading dock and with Mr. Stubblefield helping, soon they had everything. Tad picked up his rifle leaning against the wagon seat and swung it into the crook of his arm, then he walked with Mr. Stubblefield into the store to settle his bill.

Two strangers were poking around the case of rifles. One was sighting along the barrel of a new Henry. Tad had never seen the men before.

"I'll be right with you fellows," Mr. Stubblefield said. "Would there be anything else for you today, Tad?"

"Sack up a dozen sticks of that red and white candy over yonder too," Tad said. "My little sister's got herself a sweet tooth."

The storekeeper counted out the stick candy and placed the sack on the counter. He licked the end of his lead pencil and figured the bill.

"That comes to twenty-four dollars. I'll throw the candy in as boot."

Tad pulled a black, snap change purse from his pocket and took out a wad of folding money. He counted out enough to pay his bill and then stuck the rest back where it came from.

"I need a word with the sheriff, reckon he's in his office?" Tad asked.

"Saw him a little while ago. I reckon he'll be there. Did you hear we hired a new deputy? We've been short handed ever since that Dutton fellow killed Cecil Mason. A good lawman is hard to come by these days, especially in a small town like Lubbock. We got ourselves a good one, though. He's got himself quite a reputation, too. Name's Hugh Overstreet. Half of Texas call him the fastest gun alive, the rest just ain't met him yet. You ever heard of him?"

"Don't reckon I have. Don't guess I ever seen a real live gunfighter before."

"Well, he's changed his ways. Years got a way of doing that to a fellow. I'd guess him to be five years either way from fifty. He's give up gun fighting and taken up law work."

"Hey, Mister, you gonna jaw with that kid all day or you gonna wait on us?" The tall, thin fellow demanded in a gruff voice.

Tad swung a look at the speaker. The man's head set on a long neck with a protruding Adam's apple that bobbed when he swallowed. His large, beady eyes stared hard at Tad.

His partner was a big, burly looking fellow, thick through the chest and wide in the shoulders. He had black, shaggy hair and a beard to match. His teeth were tobacco-stained yellow.

"Reckon I'll mosey on over across the street," Tad said, scooping up the sack of candy and his rifle. "I'll be right back directly and head home."

Tad turned and walked out, glancing back over his shoulder at the two men. The thin one followed him with a hard gaze. Tad didn't like their looks.


George Paxton sat at his desk talking to another man when Tad pushed open the door and walked in.

"Afternoon, Tad. Didn't know you were in town," the sheriff said. "Like you to meet my new deputy, this is Hugh Overstreet. Hugh, shake hands with Tad Littlejohn."

The man that pushed himself to his feet and stuck out a friendly hand was a tall man, rangy and long boned—a hard man, Tad judged. His face was weathered down to its elements like good saddle leather. His salt and pepper hair was more salt than pepper. His face housed pale eyes that never seemed to blink and a slash of mouth that curled into something resembling a smile. He wore a Smith & Wesson .44 tied low on his left leg in a cut-away holster that was greased slick.

"The one folks are calling the Youngest Bounty Hunter in Texas, yeah, I've heard of you," the man said.

"Howdy, Mr. Overstreet," Tad said, looking the man square in the eyes as he shook the outstretched hand with a firm handshake.

"It's none of my business, Mr. Paxton," Tad said, "but there's a couple of strangers over in Mr. Stubblefield's store that was mouthing off at him. They looked like hard men to me."

"Sit tight, Sheriff," Overstreet said. "I'll check them out."

The new deputy turned and hurried out the door. Tad was surprised to see the man move with the effortless, catlike grace of a man half his age.

"He's a good man," George Paxton said when the new deputy closed the door. "He'll be a big help."

"Mr. Stubblefield tells me he was a gunfighter."

"One of the best, maybe *the* best."

"What brings him to a small, out of the way place like Lubbock?"

"I asked him that same question. He said he was just plain tired of looking over his shoulder. Said he was looking for a place where he didn't jump when he saw his own shadow."

Tad and the sheriff talked about T.J. and the funeral for several minutes.

"I reckon your pa was the best friend I ever had. We rode a lot of trails together, rode together when he was a scout for the army. We served in the Texas Rangers together. I sure will miss him."

"We all do."

The door opened and Overstreet walked back inside. "They were riding out of town before I got there. All I saw was their dust. I asked Mr. Stubblefield if they gave him any trouble. He said they were just loudmouths. He said they left right after you did."

"Good," the sheriff said. "We've had enough trouble in Lubbock lately to last a lifetime, we don't need any more. How's your mother, Tad?"

"She's doing some better. She don't cry as much anymore. Heard anything about that fellow who shot my pa?"

"No, I talked to the judge and he swore out a warrant for him."

"Will he be arrested?"

"Well, no, I doubt it, son. Warrants issued here in Texas don't mean much in New Mexico Territory. From what your pa told me about this fellow, he swings a mighty big loop in that neck of the woods."

Tad swallowed hard. Anger festered deep down inside his belly and boiled up his backbone to turn his face a crimson red. His mouth set in a thin line and his jaw muscles bulged.

"So then, it sounds like you're saying nobody is gonna do nothing about him shooting my pa in the back."

"Tad, I'm sorry, but there just ain't nothing more I can do."

"Well, there's something I can do. I'm gonna kill Buck Slade, Sheriff. Don't know when, don't know how, but I got it to do."

With that said, Tad turned on his heels and walked out the door.

"There goes a young man with a powerful mad on," Hugh Overstreet said, pouring himself a cup of leftover coffee.

"Yeah, and that wasn't just boy talk, he means to do what he said."

"But how can he? New Mexico Territory is a long way from here and even if he could get there, which would be nigh on impossible, he wouldn't stand a chance going up against a powerful man like that. Didn't you tell me this Buck Slade fellow owns a big spread and has a small army of men riding for him?"

"Yep, that's what T. J. said, but you'd have to have known his pa to understand what I'm telling you. That boy's so much like his pa it's plumb scary, he won't quit until he's done what you just heard him say, or died trying."

"Most likely be the tail end of what you said. How old did you say the boy is?"

"He's fourteen, but his pa told me more'n once that Tad was more man than most men and I reckon he wasn't far off the mark."

"Well, like the boy said, it just ain't right. Kinda makes a man want to do something to help him right a wrong."

"I know what you mean," the sheriff said.

Max Stringer and his partner, Wilbur Bonner rode northwest out of Lubbock.

"How do you know that kid will come this way?" Wilbur asked as they rode.

"Can't you see those fresh wagon tracks?" Max told him. "He came to town this way, sure enough. Likely he'll go back the same way he come in."

"Did you see that wad of greenbacks that kid was carrying? Wonder where he got that much money?"

"Who cares where he got it? In a little bit we'll have it."

"Yeah, hee-hee," Wilbur cackled. "I'm gonna get me a bottle of rye whiskey and a frisky woman with my part, what are you gonna do with yours?"

"I'm going to have a hot bath, a thick steak, and a soft bed, then decide what to do next. It was a long ride up from Abilene.

I'm tired looking over my shoulder to see if a posse's gaining on me. I want to rest up for a few days. Lubbock seems like a good place to take it easy for awhile. All we need is some money to tide us over."

"Reckon how long it will be before the kid comes?"

"What difference does it make? What else you got to do? He'll be along. Those rocks up ahead that hug both sides of the road looks like a good place for an ambush. You wait on one side and I'll take the other. Stay out of sight and keep quiet. We'll come at him from both sides at the same time."

"Yeah, we'll have him cold, hee hee. Then I'm gonna get me some whiskey and a woman.

"Just shut up about the whiskey and women, will you? I'm tired hearing it."

Tad was still upset when he climbed into his wagon. He set his rifle beside his seat and let off the brake. He popped the reins on the mule team's rumps and yelled, 'get up there, mules.' The big brown Missouri mules lunged against their harness and the heavily loaded wagon began to move.

As he drove up the street Tad nodded howdies to several people passing by and touched a finger to his floppy hat to the ladies. Soon he reached the outskirts of town and settled down for the long ride home.

As he drove, his mind replayed the conversation in the sheriff's office. He didn't blame George Paxton, he was a good sheriff, to Tad's way of thinking, but something was wrong when a man could just shoot someone in the back and nobody seemed to be able to do anything about it.

*If the judge has issued a warrant like the sheriff said, wonder if there was a wanted poster put out for Buck Slade?*

*Why wouldn't there be? He's a wanted man isn't he? Wouldn't that make him fair game for bounty hunters? What if there was a reward? Maybe even dead or alive? Now there's a thought. I might even post the reward myself and then collect my own reward money. Wouldn't that make it legal for me to kill Slade? I'll talk to the sheriff about that the next time I'm in town.*

Tad's thoughts were suddenly scattered when a rider burst from behind the rocks to his left. Another spurred from the right. Both wore bandanas pulled up over their noses and held pistols trained squarely on him.

Tad automatically grabbed for his rifle, but relaxed his grip when he found no chance to bring it up into play.

"That's a good boy," the slim one said in a gruff voice that Tad recognized from earlier in the store. "Just lift that rifle by the barrel and pitch it over here to me."

Tad had no choice but to do what the man said. The outlaw caught the rifle with his free hand while keeping his pistol aimed at Tad.

"Now climb on down, boy."

The slim one dismounted and dropped his reins to the ground as Tad climbed down from the wagon. Tad's mind raced. He flicked a glance at the big man still in his saddle nearby. He still kept his pistol out.

*What do they want?* Tad thought. *What would they want with a wagon load of feed and a cook stove?* Then he remembered the money in the change purse in his pocket. *Of course, they saw me take the money out to pay Mr. Stubblefield. They mean to rob me.*

"We want that money in your pocket, kid."

"Yeah, hee-hee, we want the money," the big fellow on his horse cackled.

They knew he carried money, there was no use pretending he didn't, so he reached into his pocket and pulled out the little black change purse and handed it to the man standing in front of him.

The outlaw opened the snaps, pulled out the folded bills, and crammed them into his pocket. Without a word he lashed out with his pistol, striking Tad alongside his right ear with a sickening blow.

The world flared hot and bright before his eyes. Pain ripped through him and surged over his body. Blackness shrouded Tad's sight. Tiny lights flickered in front of him. He felt himself falling. The ground rushed up to meet him. He landed with a jarring thud. He heard a loud blast. Something slammed into his side like a sledgehammer. Another blast seemed far off in the distance. Another jarring blow tore into his body.

And then a soft blackness wrapped its arms around him.

# Chapter III

"Let's mosey over to the café and surround some supper," George Paxton said, pushing from his chair and snatching his hat from the wall peg.

"You buying?" Hugh Overstreet kidded.

"On what they pay me I can barely afford to buy my own, much less yours, besides, I've already took note of how much you can eat. For a thin fellow, you sure can put it away."

They stepped down off the boardwalk and headed across the street. A strong, chilly wind was blowing in from the north. George set his hat on his head and tugged it down tight. The blood-red sun ball was inching close to the western horizon. Streaks of gold and white splayed across the sky.

A large freight wagon barreled down the street toward them; the teamster hollared and whipped his two-hitch team, urging them to greater speed.

The two lawmen scrambled out of the way as the big wagon lumbered to a stop in a cloud of dust.

"Sheriff," the teamster shouted. "There's a boy in the back

of the wagon. I come upon him a couple of miles out of town. Looks like somebody jumped him. He's shot up pretty bad."

George and Hugh rushed to the back of the wagon. The sheriff took one look.

"It's Tad Littlejohn! Quick, go get the doctor."

The sheriff pressed his hand against Tad's throat, searching for a pulse. He finally found one ,but it was weak. The front of Tad's shirt was soaked with blood. Two bullet holes had punched through the boy's shirt. An ugly gash along his right cheek and a black eye that was swollen shut told George the boy had been pistol whipped, most likely before he was shot.

Folks heard the commotion and began gathering around. Wiley Stubblefield hurried up.

"Who is it, George? What's happened?"

"It's Tad Littlejohn. Somebody's shot him and left him on the road for dead. He might near is too."

The doctor rushed up carrying his little black bag. He took a quick look, felt Tad's pulse, and turned to the sheriff.

"Get him over to my office. Hurry, he's hurt bad."

Somebody came up with a canvas tarp. They spread it on the ground and carefully lifted Tad onto it. Four men hurried him to the doctor's office. George and Hugh followed closely behind.

"I'm gonna stay with the boy," George told his new deputy. "How about you riding out and taking a look around before it gets too dark. Take someone with you in case Tad's wagon and team are still there."

Without a word the deputy whirled and trotted toward the livery, calling out to a man standing nearby to come with him.

\* \* \*

Time seemed to drag by. George Paxton paced the floor, pulling out his watch and glancing at it every few minutes. Wiley Stubblefield was there. So were Reverend Hensley and a dozen others. All sat in hushed silence.

Outside the wind howled. George wrestled with himself in his mind. He knew that Mary would have been expecting Tad home before dark. She would be worried sick.

Just before nine o'clock Hugh Overstreet opened the door and motioned the sheriff outside.

"How's the boy?"

"He's still alive, but barely. The doctor got the bullets out. He's bad, but the doctor said if he can hold on until morning he still has a chance. What did you find out there?"

"The boy's wagon and team was there. We brought it back to town. It's down at the livery.

"It was two men. They waited behind the rocks and came at him from both sides. The boy didn't have a chance. The strange thing is their tracks led right back here into town."

"You mean somebody from town did this?"

"I stopped by the saloon and had a word with the bar keep. He said two strangers stopped in earlier today. The barman said they barely had enough money to buy a beer this afternoon, but they seemed to be flush tonight.

"He said one of them bought a bottle and was upstairs with one of the girls right now. The other one is over at the hotel in a hot tub of water."

"Let's go."

The two lawmen walked side by side up the dusty street. Wind kicked up dust that swirled around their feet and legs. Out of habit from long years of living on the edge, their eyes flicked to and fro, searching for any unseen danger.

"You take the one in the saloon," George told his deputy. "I'll take the one in the hotel."

George Paxton was mad. He had been a lawman a long time. Usually he didn't let things get personal; this time was different. Somebody was gonna pay for what they done to the boy.

His long strides carried him to the hotel. He pushed through the door and crossed the lobby with long gaited steps toward the stairs. Over a shoulder he called out to Ben Longtree, the night man, who was sitting behind the counter reading a newspaper.

"A stranger checked in this afternoon. What room is he in?"

"Like I told the new deputy, he's in room number six, first room upstairs on the right. He's soaking in a bath right now."

George was already headed up the stairs two at a time before the desk clerk got the words out. He lifted his pistol from its holster and thumbed back the hammer as he reached the top of the stairs. He turned right and stopped outside the door to room number six.

Lifting a booted foot he kicked the door in. It splintered and flew from its hinges. George followed what was left of the door into the room.

A naked man sat in a soapy tub of water with a startled look on his face. His eyes were wide and his mouth was open as if to say something. He grabbed for the pistol in a holster hanging on a nearby chair.

"Go ahead," George said in a voice low and menacing. "Give me an excuse to blow your head plumb off your shoulders."

The fellow slowly withdrew his hand.

"I ought to blow your brains out right where you sit. Which one of you pistol whipped and shot the boy?"

"What...what boy? I don't know what you're talking about"

"You lying piece of garbage!"

George Paxton lost his cool. He took a step closer, grabbed a handful of hair, yanked the man's head back, and pressed the nose of his cocked pistol against the outlaw's forehead, right between the eyes.

"I ain't asking again."

"Okay, okay, it was Bonner. He just went crazy. I didn't want to hurt the kid. It was him that done it."

"Get up and get your pants on. If you so much as twitch, I'll blow your filthy heart through your backbone."

Deputy Hugh Overstreet shoved through the batwing doors of the saloon. A sweeping glance of the room told him that his man must still be upstairs. He flicked a look at the bar man. The bar jockey pointed a stubby finger upstairs.

The deputy climbed the stairs and stopped outside the first room. He pressed his ear to the door. Not a sound. He moved on down the hall to the second door.

A woman's laughter came from inside. A man's voice spoke.

"What'cha doin? Come on back to bed, hee-hee, I ain't finished yet."

"I'm pouring us another drink, baby. Keep your shirt on. Oh, I forgot, darling, you don't have a shirt on do you?" She laughed again.

Hugh kicked the door in.

The woman stood in front of the dresser pouring drinks from a half-empty bottle. She was completely naked.

A big, burly man with a black beard and wearing only his dirty, faded-red long john bottoms and boots lay on the rumpled bed. A pistol in a worn holster hung on the bedpost.

Before the man could even move the deputy was across the room. His hand flashed. A pistol appeared as if by magic. Pale half-light from the single lamp reflected off the barrel of the Smith & Wesson as it scribed a wide arc.

The vicious blow smashed into the bridge of the big outlaw's nose with such force it sent him tumbling out of the bed. The big, bearded man lay stunned on the floor, his nose shattered and blood spurting from his nostrils.

The deputy shot a sideways glance at the girl. She stood unmoving, her hand covering her mouth in shocked disbelief.

Reaching a hand, Hugh gathered a handful of the long, black hair and hoisted the man to his feet. He half-dragged him through the shattered door and down the hall. When he reached the top of the stairs he flung the man down them.

Over and over the big man tumbled, coming to a stop in a crumpled heap on the floor of the saloon. Customers scattered. The bearded man groaned and tried to get up, finally managing to climb unsteadily to one knee.

Hugh Overstreet was there. A boot lashed out, landing square in the big man's open mouth. Blood and teeth splayed in every direction. The man tumbled over backwards.


Mary paced the porch, lifting her eyes every few steps to stare off into the darkness toward the creek. A white shawl hugged her shoulders. Dread coiled inside her stomach, twisting and writhing like a snake. Fear, and grief, and the edge of panic blossomed in her chest and gnawed its way up into her throat. Ruthless, icy fingers tugged at her heart.

A blustery, cold wind howled through the trees and tore at her hair and clothes, chilling her to the bone. Yet she paid it no mind and kept pacing.

"Come inside, Mother," Marilyn pleaded. "It's freezing out here. You'll be sick."

Not trusting her voice Mary only shook her head.

*What could have happened?* Mary's troubled mind screamed out for an answer. *He said he would be back before dark. Something bad has happened to my son, I can feel it. Should I send Lupe to find him? Should I go myself? Should I wait until morning or go tonight?*

Finally, her body shaking, her teeth chattering, and chilled to the very marrow of her bones, Mary reluctantly allowed them to help her inside. Lupe stoked up the fire. Marilyn scooted the rocker up close to the fire and draped a quilt around her mother's shaking shoulders.

"I'll make some coffee," Marilyn said.


It was raining in the Littlejohn valley, a cold, persistent drizzle that wrapped the world in a gray haze and made the coming of day a hard-fought dawn. The rain matched the mood of the occupants who lay on pallets scattered around the dying embers of a neglected fire.

Only Mary kept the lonely vigil. She shivered from the dampness and clutched the large family bible from which she sought comfort during the long, lonely night. Her unblinking gaze fixed absently on its open pages.

*Why, Lord? Why do You allow bad things to happen to good people? What elusive purpose was served by taking my husband and the father of our children from us? And now, another tragedy has been visited upon us. Something bad has happened to my son. His spirit cries out to me. What can I do? Where can I turn if not to You? Help me . . . please help me.*

Outside Shep barked, alerting them that someone was approaching.

"Hello, the house!" the male voice from outside interrupted Mary's musings.

Casting aside the quilt from her shoulders, she pushed anxiously from the rocking chair and rushed to the front door.

"Mary, it's George Paxton."

Mary's fingers fumbled hurriedly lifted the wooden bar from the front door and swung the door open wide. He stood there, water dripping from the rain-soaked hat and slicker and looking every bit like the guardian angel she prayed for.

Dim light from the single lamp inside fell on a troubled face. His look confirmed her greatest fear. His arms opened, offering comfort. She accepted and allowed them to clutch her close.

For a long moment all was well with the world. For a fleeting blink of eternity she felt safe, comforted, and loved.

She lifted her eyes to his. Her eyes asking the question before the words were uttered.

"What has happened to my son?" She asked.

"He's alive. He's been hurt. But he's alive."

"Where is he? I've got to go to him."

"I borrowed the buckboard from Doctor Gattis. Bring a quilt to wrap yourself in, it's getting colder. My new deputy rode out with me to stay with the children."

For the first time Mary realized another man stood on the porch behind the sheriff and she hadn't even invited them inside.

"Come in, I'll get my things, I won't be a minute."

George and Hugh removed their hats and shook the water from them, then stepped inside the dimly lit room. Mary disappeared into another room. The three children huddled together under quilts near the stove, sound asleep.

George moved quietly across the room to the wood box. It was nearly empty. He lifted the last two sticks and opened the squeaky door to the stove. Taking up a nearby poker, he stoked the dying coals and then placed the wood inside.

"Hugh, how about getting an armload of wood from that wood pile beside the house?"

Marilyn raised her head from the pallet, rubbed sleepy eyes with a fist and climbed from her warm covers.

"Morning, Mr. Paxton. Is my brother okay?"

"He's been hurt. I'm taking your mother to see him. She will explain."

"I'll make some fresh coffee," she said, climbing to her bare feet.

"Coffee sure would go good on a cold morning like this," he said.

Hugh filled the wood box to overflowing while Mary rushed around the house, gathering what she would need for the trip into town. George stood close to the stove, warming his cold hands.

"Marilyn, you'll have to fix the children breakfast," Mary said as she hurriedly stuffed things into a worn-out valise. "You and Lupe will have to see to things here, I don't know when I will be back."

"Don't worry, Mother, we'll be fine, just take care of Tad."

The ride to town was long, wet, and cold. Mary huddled inside the quilt and clutched it close. George spread a canvas tarp over their legs up to the waist to repel the steady drizzle.

As they drove, George explained as best he could what had happened.

"It seems Tad was waylaid by two drifters that happened to see the money when Tad paid Wiley Stubblefield for the feed. They were broke and needed what he had. They were willing to kill him for it."

"What kind of men would do something like that?"

"Bad men. Some men are just plumb bad to the bone. They don't care about nothing or nobody but themselves. They take what they want no matter who they have to hurt to get it."

For a long while they rode in silence.

"George . . . do you think Tad is going to be all right?"

"I believe so, Mary. I believe so."

*God how he wished he really believed what he had just told her.*

# Chapter IV

For two days and nights Mary sat by the bedside of her unconscious son. At times fever ran rampant in his young body, sweat drenching the sheets of his bed. At those times Mary gently pressed a wet cloth to his fevered brow and bathed his bruised and swollen face with love.

Other times his body shook violently with cold chills. She piled quilts on and around him and, as a last resort, climbed into the bed with her son, using the heat from her own body to warm his.

Others came and went: Reverend Hensley, Wiley and Doris Stubblefield, Jed and Adelaide Holly drove all the way into town to see if there was something they could do to help. Some from the church brought soup and well wishes.

The sheriff walked up to the cell holding the slimmer of the two prisoners and stood, staring through the bars at the outlaw. The man stared back defiantly.

"Step back over against the back wall and don't move if you want supper."

The man stood unmoving for a long minute. Finally, he stepped away from the bars and moved to the back wall.

George Paxton inserted a large key and unlocked the door. He set the tray of food on the floor and swung the door closed, turned the key, and then shook the door to make sure it was securely locked.

"When am I gonna get to see a lawyer?"

"You best worry about that boy living. If he dies, I'm gonna hang you, lawyer or no lawyer."

"What about what that deputy done to me?" The big, bearded man in the next cell yelled. "He had no call to do me like he did."

"You got more to worry about than a few missing teeth and a broken nose. If your mama taught you how to pray, you better be talking to Him about sparing that boy's life. I might just decide to leave you alone with my deputy for awhile before we hang you."

"That deputy of yours is a crazy man. He's mean as a den full of rattlers. He oughta be locked up instead of me."

"Oh, not that it matters much now, but I got a telegram from down Abilene way. Seems you boys have been busy. You're both wanted for robbery down there too."

"Weren't us."

"Of course not," the sheriff said, turning and walking back into his office and slamming the heavy wooden door behind him.

Mary was thankful for George. She enjoyed his company. His presence made her feel safe. He was a good friend. She didn't know what she would have done without him during this time.

It was one of those times when George and Mary were sitting together, talking quietly, that Mary saw Tad's one good eyelid flutter, then blink open. Mary leaped from the chair.

"Did you see that? He's waking up. George, he's waking up."

George Paxton saw it too. He pushed quickly from the chair to stand beside Mary. She leaned to press her cheek to her son's.

"Where...where am I?" Tad muttered through cracked and swollen lips. "What happened?"

"You've been hurt, son. Just lie still and don't move. You're going to be all right."

A relieved look settled over Tad's face. He closed his eyes again and drifted off into a peaceful sleep.

Without realizing what he was doing, George lifted an arm to surround Mary's shoulders in an act of comfort.

Tears of thankfulness seeped from Mary's eyes. An overwhelming sense of relief surged through her. She drew a deep, shaky breath and, becoming aware for the first time of the strong arm around her shoulders, lifted her eyes to find his.

Something, she wasn't quite sure what, passed between them. She had come to depend upon this strong, but gentle man whose arm felt so good around her. She felt a growing closeness with the man who'd been such a good friend to her husband.

*What was it T.J. said to George in those final moments just before his life slipped away? "Watch after my family," he told his friend, to which George replied, "You can count on it."*

A soft tap on the door jarred her mind back to the present. She felt George's arm quickly move from around her.

"Come in," she called softly so as not to wake Tad.

It was Homer and Henrietta Green, their closest neighbors that lived only a few miles from the Littlejohn valley.

"We just heard about it this morning or we would have been here sooner," Henrietta explained. "Jed Holly rode over and told us about what happened."

"Thanks for coming," Mary said, stepping over to hug her friend.

"How's Tad?"

"He just woke up a few minutes ago. He's been unconscious for three days."

"That's wonderful news."

"I hear you caught the ones that done it," Homer said, looking at the sheriff.

"Yep. They're over in jail."

"Well, I hope the judge locks them up and throws away the key. Don't know what the world's coming to these days."

"We drove by your house to check on the children," Henrietta said. "That new deputy seems to have everything under control out there. He seems like such a nice sort of fellow."

"He's a good man," George said.

"Mary, is there anything you need?" Henrietta asked. "Is there anything we can do to help?"

"Thanks, but no, all we need is for Tad to get well."

"How long did the doctor say he will be laid up?"

"He said that he shouldn't be moved for at least two weeks. After that we should be able to move him home to continue his recovery."

"Well, we best be going. If there is anything we can do you will send word, won't you?"

"I will," Mary said. "Thank you both for coming."

* * *

*It feels good,* Hugh Overstreet thought. *Being out here with the kids and all feels kinda like it did before my own family was murdered.*

That was nearly twenty years ago. But not a day passed in all that time that he hadn't thought about them. It still hurt to remember.

*A little spread in south Texas, not much different from this one. A few head of cattle, a small two-room cabin, snug and warm and dry. A beautiful wife. A ten year old daughter as pretty as a ray of morning sunshine. All gone. All taken away by a gang of murdering scum that rode in, raped my wife and daughter, then rode away while I was out chasing stray cattle.*

*It took three years, but I found every single one of them. I shot them down like the dogs they were. After that, the die was cast, my reputation as a gunfighter was sealed. Every would-be punk that thought he was fast with a gun came looking for me. It was kill or be killed.*

"Are you okay, Mr. Hugh?" Lupe asked with a look of concern occupying his face.

"Huh? Oh, yeah, son, I'm okay. I was just thinking about something. You ready to saw some more logs?"

They spent the last two days sawing up the last of the logs Lupe and Tad snaked in earlier. They worked from sunup until sundown, stopping only when Marilyn called them in for lunch and dinner.

Even on a small spread like this one, Hugh had forgotten how much work it took to keep things going: They milked the cow, slopped the hogs, fed the chickens, forked hay out of the loft for the cattle and horses, mended fences, and on and on and on. It was a good life. He had forgotten how good.

"Can I ask you something?" Lupe asked as they loaded another log onto the cross stands.

"You can ask me anything."

"Are you good with that pistol you wear?"

"Some say I am."

"Have you ... have you ever killed anybody with it?"

His answer was a long time coming.

"I'm sorry to say I have. More than once, I'm afraid. Fact is, son, I wish I'd never strapped on a gun. Once a man straps on a gun it changes him."

"I would never let it change me," Lupe said.

"It's a bad idea, son, you'd be better off to forget about it."

"I'm going to kill a man."

"Whoa, now, that's not something to joke about."

"I'm very serious, *señor*."

"Who is this man you're going to kill and why do you want to kill him?"

"It is the man that killed Mr. Littlejohn. I will kill him because if I don't Tad will try to do it and he will get killed. Tad is my friend."

"So, let me get this straight, you are going to try to kill this man to keep your friend from getting killed, is that right?"

"*Si.*"

"Is this the fellow down in New Mexico Territory we're talking about?"

Lupe nodded his reply.

"And just *how* do you intend to do this?"

"With the pistol. I will learn to shoot the pistol and I will kill him."

"Have you ever shot a pistol?"

"Once, I killed an Apache that was trying to kill Mr. Littlejohn."

"You did? I see. Well, if you're dead-set on learning to use a pistol, I suppose I'll teach you all I can. Maybe we could find time after we get these logs sawed up to ride down by the creek and see how good you are."

"Really? Could we? Will you teach me how to shoot?"

"Well, let's get these logs sawed up first, then we'll see."

True to his word, that afternoon Hugh and Lupe saddled their horses and rode down to the creek beside the big oak tree. They tied their horses and Hugh unbuckled his saddlebag. Reaching inside, he pulled out a holster with the gun belt wrapped around it. Inside the holster was a Smith & Wesson .44, identical to the one he kept strapped around his waist.

He handed the holster and pistol to his young friend.

"Before we start there's some things I want you to think about. Guns are made for one thing and one thing only, to kill people with. I want you to think about that. If you can't settle your mind around that, then you got no business carrying a pistol. All it will do is get you killed. You sure you're ready to look a man in the eye and kill him?"

"I'd be ready to kill Buck Slade."

"The trouble is, son, it won't stop with Buck Slade. Once you get a reputation as a gun hand there's always somebody out there that thinks by killing you he'll inherit your reputation. The sad thing is it's true, and they'll dog your trail until they give you a try. I've lived the life. I know what I'm talking about. You sure that's the kind of life you want, son?"

For a long gathering of moments Lupe studied the ground at his feet, and then lifted his eyes and nodded his head.

"Strap that around you waist and cinch it up tight."

Hugh watched as the boy followed instructions.

"Now, tie that leather thong around your leg. That keeps

the holster from riding up when you draw the pistol out. That's it, good."

"Lift the pistol out and make sure it's empty. It should be, but always assume a gun is loaded until you know for sure it isn't."

He showed the boy how to open the loading gate and spin the cylinder while looking into the six chambers to make sure there were no bullets inside.

"Now, set the pistol back into the holster lightly, never jam it down hard. You want it to slide out easy when you draw it.

"Do what I tell you real slow, okay? Lift the pistol out of the holster real slow, as it slides out let your thumb drag the hammer back. That pistol has been altered so that the hammer comes back real easy. Try it."

The boy did as Hugh instructed. At first Lupe was slow and awkward. For the better part of two hours they worked. Over and over Lupe drew the weapon, his thumb dragging back the hammer as the pistol cleared the holster.

Hugh showed the boy how to stand, how to let his arm relax and hang with his fingers hovering just below the butt of the pistol, how to keep his head still when his arm moved, and his eyes fixed straight ahead.

"I think that's enough for today," Hugh told his young friend. "You did real good."

"Can we do it again tomorrow?" Lupe asked excitedly.

"Don't see why not. Right now we better get back to work. We've still got chores to do."

*The boy's a quick learner,* Hugh thought as he toed a stirrup and swung a leg over his saddle.


For the next two weeks they rode out to the creek and practiced every day. After the first week the boy was showing amazing speed. On the seventh day Hugh allowed Lupe to load the pistol.

"It's no different than what you've been doing all along," he told the boy. "Just draw and aim like you were pointing your finger, just like I showed you. Don't jerk the trigger, squeeze it real easy-like.

"The first few times you will probably flinch when the pistol fires, don't worry about it, that's natural, you'll get over it. Are you ready? Slow at first, just lift the pistol, aim it, and squeeze the trigger."

It was like he was seeing himself all over again. He remembered all those hours and hours of practice out behind the barn when he was young, not much older than Lupe.

By the end of the second week Lupe was faster and a better shot than ninety percent of men that walked around with a pistol on their hip.

"You are coming along right good," Hugh told Lupe as they were riding back to the house. "Just keep at it, keep practicing. What you've learned so far is the easiest part. Tomorrow we start on the hard stuff."

That night after supper they made cookies. It was Marilyn that suggested it. They all joined in and helped with the mixing, stirring, and baking. Then they sat around the table and played checkers, ate cookies, and laughed. It was a happy time. One Hugh Overstreet had missed for the past twenty years.

Down at the creek the next afternoon, as Lupe swung the gun belt around his thin waist, Hugh lifted the boy's pistol from its holster and spun the cylinder to make sure it was empty. Then he did the same with his own weapon.

"Today we start on the part that separates the living gun fighters from the dead ones. Being able to draw fast and shoot straight is the easy part. Anybody can learn to do that with enough practice.

"Lots of men I've faced were faster than me, but I'm alive and they're buried in an unmarked grave in Boot Hill. What I'm about to show you most men never live long enough to learn.

"I want you to stand facing me about ten feet apart. That's how close you need to be to kill a man. If you're facing a man and he stops further than that from you, just keep walking until you are ten feet from him before you stop.

"When you face a man watch his eyes. Never take your eyes off his. His eyes will tell you when he's about to draw—that's your edge. If you know when he's about to draw before he does it, that gives you a split second on him."

"What do I look for in his eyes that tell me that?"

"In that instant when the man's brain makes the decision to draw, and even before that decision is sent to the hand to start the draw, the decision shows up in his eyes. It may be the slightest narrowing of the eyes, sometimes the eyebrows lower, sometimes the eyes widen, it's different from man to man, but you'll know. Let me show you what I mean."

Hugh and Lupe stood ten feet apart facing one another. Each dropped into the 'gun fighter's stance', feet set comfortably apart, knees slightly bent, shoulders square, arm relaxed.

"Now, anytime you are ready I want you to draw."

For a fleeting moment they stood facing each other. Suddenly Lupe's hand streaked up with the pistol in it. His weapon hadn't cleared leather before the Smith & Wesson appeared in Hugh Overstreet's hand.

Lupe couldn't believe it. He hadn't even seen his friend draw. If that had been a real gunfight he would be dead.

*"Madre Por Dios!"* Lupe exclaimed. "You must be the fastest man alive!"

"No, you just told me when you were about to draw before you did it. You narrowed your eyes. Let's do it again, this time *you* watch *my* eyes."

Over and over they practiced. Lupe quickly got the hang of it. By the end of their practice session, Lupe was reading the telegraphed message of Hugh's eyes and come close to beating him to the draw a few times.

"Like I said before, there's only one reason to ever pull a gun, son, and that's to kill the other fellow before he kills you. When a man gives you no other choice, kill him. If you don't he's gonna kill you.

"When you shoot a man, never, never, shoot him just once. The first shot almost never kills a man, and a wounded man can still kill you. When you shoot, shoot him square in the chest and keep shooting until he stops moving.

"Another thing, never let the other fellow get the idea you are scared of him. That will build his confidence and *that* will get you killed. Get your own bluff in on him if you can. Tell him in no uncertain terms what you are gonna do to him and how you are gonna do it. Then do it. Never run a bluff that you aren't ready to back up."

# Chapter V

Hugh Overstreet and Lupe were splitting wood. Marilyn had just finished hanging out a washing, and little Sally swung in her tree swing.

Shep raised his big head, looked off into the distance, and growled a low, rumbling warning.

"Somebody's coming!" Sally hollered at the top of her childish voice.

They all jerked a look toward the hill just beyond the creek. Sure enough, a wagon topped the hill and started down the near side. Another wagon followed in its tracks.

Hugh palmed the flat of his hand above his eyes to shade the noontime sun.

"That looks like the sheriff driving the first wagon. Your ma is sitting beside him. Don't recognize who's driving the other wagon."

"That's Silas Isaacs, the hostler from the livery," Lupe said.

"Where's Tad?" Marilyn asked anxiously. "I don't see him."

"Maybe he stayed in town," Hugh suggested. "Or maybe he's lying in the back of the first wagon, looks like the second wagon is loaded with feed."

They watched as the wagons crossed the creek and drew closer to the house, unable to stand it any longer, Marilyn and little Sally ran to meet them. Mary climbed down from her wagon seat and ran to meet her children, opening her arms and gathering them in.

"Don't I even get a howdy?" Tad hollered from his makeshift bed in the back of the wagon.

His sisters quickly climbed over the tailgate and showered their brother with kisses and hugs. Lupe stood watching, and then reached out a hand. Tad took it and the two friends shook hands—like brothers.

Once they had carried Tad from the wagon bed into the house to his own bed, they all sat around the kitchen table sipping the fresh pot of coffee Marilyn had made, eating another batch of cookies, and talking.

"The doctor says he will have to stay in bed another two or three weeks before it will be safe for him to get up and move around," Mary explained. "He's afraid the wounds will open up and start bleeding again."

"How did you make it actually doing an honest day's work?" George asked his deputy.

"Work, who said he did any work?" Marilyn kidded, slanting a look at Hugh.

"Just like I figured," George said. "You've been on vacation for three weeks and I've been doing my work and yours too."

"It's been tough," Hugh said, going along with the kidding. "These kids have about driven me crazy."

Marilyn threw a dishtowel at him and everybody laughed. It was a good homecoming.

"Lupe is learning to be a gun fighter," Sally informed everyone.

George flicked an inquiring look at his deputy. Mary did likewise. Lupe beamed from ear to ear, hearing himself addressed as a gun fighter for the first time.

"I was just showing the boy a few things, that's all," Hugh explained.

"Well, it's good to be home," Mary said, flicking a quick glance and a smile in George's direction.

"We better get that wagon unloaded," the sheriff said quickly. "I expect Mary and Marilyn will want to try out that new stove."

"Would you men consider staying for dinner?" Mary asked. "Like you said, we need to try it out."

"I think we could manage that. Couldn't we fellows?"

"If you're asking for my vote, you've got it. I've already sampled Marilyn's cooking. If she learned from her mother I can't wait until supper time."

The liveryman readily agreed.

George, Hugh, Lupe and Silas made short work of unloading Mary's new stove and hooking it up to the stovepipe. Then they backed the wagon into the barn and unloaded the feed.

The day was unusually warm for late fall and the men spent some time sitting on the front porch while smoking and talking. The big German Shepard lay beside them. The sweet-smelling aroma of sizzling steaks, fried potatoes, and boiled cabbage wafted through the late afternoon air and made their mouths water.

The evening sun slowly sank behind the western horizon, framing the large pine trees on the hill. Cattle were lowing, the horses were grazing peacefully, and the happy sounds of laughter from the kitchen made Hugh Overstreet shake his head.

"It just don't get any better than this, *amigo*"

For a long minute George Paxton said nothing. He just sat and soaked it all up. Finally he gave a single nod.

"Yep, you can sure say that again."

"Are you men going to sit out there all night and let this delicious supper go to waste?" Mary asked from the doorway.

"No way, no how," Hugh said, unfolding his tall frame from the chair.

They all gathered around the table except for Tad. George and Hugh carried him in, mattress and all, so he could be a part of the special homecoming supper.

When everyone was seated, Mary sat at the head of the table with George, Hugh, and Silas next in line on each side, then Lupe, Marilyn, and Sally.

Mary asked if she could ask the blessing. Everyone joined hands and bowed their heads.

Mary cleared her throat, swallowed hard, and released George's hand long enough to wipe a tear.

"Our Father which art in Heaven:

Thank You for our answered prayer. Forgive me for my doubts and questions. Thank You for good and faithful friends and for this food. Watch over and protect our loved ones.

In the name of Jesus we pray, amen."

Just before they raised their heads, Mary felt George squeeze her hand tightly. She felt it all the way to her heart.

After supper, George, Hugh, and Silas hitched up the team to the extra wagon and saddled up Hugh's horse. As he was tightening his cinch strap, Lupe walked into the barn.

"I wanted to say thanks for showing me what you did," he said, sticking out his hand.

Hugh took the offered hand and shook it. Then turned to his saddlebags and pulled out the gun rig Lupe had been using.

"Here, I want you to have this."

"I couldn't accept that, Mr. Hugh, it's worth no telling how much. I could never afford anything that nice."

"It's yours, use it wisely."

On the way back to town later that night, George asked the question Hugh knew would be coming.

"What's this about you teaching Lupe to use a gun?"

"The way it came about there was just no way I could tell him no. He's made up his mind that he's gonna kill Buck Slade to keep Tad from trying to do it. He's convinced Slade will kill Tad, and he's most likely right. Lupe is willing to take the chance of getting himself killed in order to save Tad.

"Seems I recollect something from the bible that says something about 'Greater love has no man than this, that he lay down his life for his friend.' That is exactly what Lupe has in mind, I was just trying to even up the odds a bit."

"Do you think he will actually try to do what he says?"

"I'm convinced he will. George, I've seen lots of fast guns in my time, this kid has the makings of one of the best. He's come farther in three weeks than most men do in a lifetime."

"Well, if he's as good as you say, most likely you haven't done him any favors. You know better than anyone what the life of a man with a reputation as a fast gun is like."

"That's true, but I believe I might have just saved his life too."

The weeks slipped slowly by. Tad had regained his appetite and was eating like it was his last meal. He gained strength rapidly. Soon the big day came when Mary agreed to allow him to sit in the rocker by the fire. It was the day before Christmas.

"I'm sorry, Ma, but I didn't get a chance to get any of you anything for Christmas."

"Tad, just seeing you able to be up and around is the greatest gift I could hope for."

Lupe came in that afternoon with a small Cedar tree he had found up on the East Ridge. Everyone was excited about having a real Christmas tree. They all joined in decorating it.

It was Christmas Day. The sun was halfway to high. George Paxton waded his big gray gelding across the creek and reined to a stop under the big oak tree near T.J.'s grave. He sat his saddle and stared for a long minute at the mound of dirt and the wooden cross at the head of the grave.

He missed his old friend; they had been saddle pards for a long time. He felt a tinge of guilt at the feelings he was having for Mary. He wouldn't do anything in the world to betray the friendship he and T.J. had but his friend's last words to him kept ringing in his mind, 'watch after my family' T.J. had asked of him.

*Am I looking for something in that last request that wasn't meant? Am I looking for an excuse to feel what I'm feeling? Is it just me, or does Mary feel something too? Sure wish I knew how to play the hand I've been dealt.*

Lately he hadn't been able to get Mary off his mind. He seemed drawn to her like a moth to a flame. Her long, golden hair that she wore gathered in a bun on the back of her head, those beautiful eyes, the color of a summer sky, those full, pouting lips that he'd trade his soul to kiss, all those memories haunted him day and night.

Those three weeks Mary had spent at Tad's bedside in the hotel had given George an excuse to be with her. He had used every opportunity to drop by and spend an hour or so at least twice every day.

Twisting a look, he stared for a long minute at the Littlejohn cabin off in the distance. A thin tendril of smoke rose from the stovepipe and drifted lazily upward against a sloping mountain backdrop thick with towering pine trees. It was a pretty scene that warmed his heart.

Touching heels to his mount, he short-loped the quarter mile to the house. Shep trotted out to meet him, wagging his tail. He reined up near the corral. Lupe saw him from the barn and walked out to meet him. George noticed the boy was wearing the gun rig Hugh had given him. It looked natural on him, like he had been born with it around his waist.

"Morning, Mr. Paxton."

"Morning to you, Lupe, and Merry Christmas."

George swung a leg over the saddle and settled it to the ground. He untied the tow sack full of presents from behind his saddle and swung them over a shoulder.

"I'll unsaddle your horse and turn him into the corral," Lupe volunteered.

"Thanks. I'll mosey on up to the house and see if I can talk Mary out of a cup of coffee."

George felt like Santa Clause walking to the house with a tow sack full of gifts slung over his shoulder. He had spent a good part of his whole month's salary, but that was okay, the excitement he felt deep inside his chest made the cost a small thing. Stepping onto the porch he knocked on the heavy front door.

The door swung open and Mary stood there. Her mouth flew open with surprise and her face lit up like a Christmas tree.

"George Paxton. What a wonderful surprise. What are you doing way out here on Christmas Day?"

"Well, ma'am, old Santa Clause was in something of a hurry last night and asked me if I would mind dropping this sack full of presents off for the Littlejohn family. Course, I couldn't say no to a jolly old fellow like that."

"Of course not, come on in, George, it's good to see you."

"It's good to see you too, Mary. Merry Christmas."

For a fleeting instant their eyes met, and held. Mary broke a soft smile. George felt his face flush crimson. Mary stepped aside to let him in.

Tad was sitting in a rocking chair near the big stove.

"There's leftover coffee if you'd like a cup?" Mary said.

"Leftover would be fine, thanks. Morning, Tad, Merry Christmas."

"Morning, Mr. Paxton."

"How you coming along, son?"

"Good I reckon. I'm way past ready to be up and around though."

"I can imagine. I'm sure it's hard for an active young man like you to have to stay in bed."

"Sure is, I hear you caught the men that shot me?"

Mary handed George a steaming cup of coffee. He glanced up at her from the straight-backed chair. She was looking at him. He wrinkled a smile. Mary blushed and quickly turned away.

"Yeah, the judge set their trial for the first week in February," he said, blowing away the steam and taking a sip.

"What kind of time do you reckon they'll get?"

"If I had my way about it, they'd get life, but it'll be up to a jury to decide."

"Mr. Paxton," Sally said, walking in from her bedroom. "Are those presents for me?"

"Well, I think I remember Santa Clause saying there was something there for Sally Littlejohn, is that you?"

""Mr. Paxton, you're joshing me, you know who I am."

"Then I reckon there might just be something there for you. Would you want to take them presents out of the sack and put them under the tree?"

He didn't have to ask twice. Sally ran across the room and started pulling the Christmas-wrapped presents from the sack and searching for one with her name on it.

"I've been thinking on something, Sheriff. I got a question to ask," Tad asked.

"Let's hear it."

"You said when we were talking the other day that the judge had sworn out a warrant for Buck Slade, right?"

"That's right."

"Does that mean there is a wanted poster out on him?"

"Well, no, I suppose there could be though. We just never had one made up and distributed."

"Why not?"

"Well, it's like I said, warrants issued in Texas don't mean much down in New Mexico Territory."

"How does it work when there is a reward offered for somebody? Who puts up that reward?"

"Sometimes, if the fellow is a particularly bad hombre, the state puts up the reward. Other times some company, like Wells-Fargo, or the railroad, or a bank, posts a reward. Sometimes even individuals offer a reward for someone's capture."

"Is there any reason I couldn't post a reward on Buck Slade?"

"You? Well, uh, I ain't sure. I can't think of anything that would keep you from it if you was of a mind."

"I'm of a mind. I'd like to offer a five hundred dollar reward for Buck Slade, dead or alive."

"Whoa, now as to the 'dead or alive' I'm not sure the judge would go along with that."

"Why wouldn't he? Buck Slade shot my pa in the back. Lots of folk saw him do it. Isn't that murder?"

"Yeah, that's murder, sure enough. Let me give it some thought, Tad. Maybe you've come up with something here."

"Will you let me know what you find out?"

"You can lay odds on it."

"George," Mary said from the kitchen, "You are staying for dinner. I won't take no for an answer. Lupe shot a wild turkey and I'm baking it in my new stove. We're having sweet potatoes, turnips, and we've got yeast rolls rising."

"Best offer I've had today."

*It feels like home,* George thought, as he watched the children open their presents. *I'm just beginning to realize how much I've missed this.*

It had been a wonderful meal. Mary and Marilyn had outdone themselves. George ate until he couldn't eat any more, then Mary went to the oven and produced a pumpkin pie.

It was twilight before he finally told everyone goodbye, wished them a merry Christmas, and climbed into the saddle for the long ride back to town.

For most of the twenty- mile ride George thought about Mary and how much he enjoyed the day. But something else also weighed on his mind. Over and over he considered the questions Tad had asked about the wanted poster on Buck Slade and why there wasn't one. He decided that he was going to talk to the judge about the subject, and he was going to do it first thing Monday morning when the judge got into his office.

# Chapter VI

The next two months passed swiftly. Tad was totally healed. The worst part of winter was passed. The two outlaws that had attacked Tad had been tried, found guilty as charged, and sentenced to ten years hard labor.

Tad knew, of course that Lupe had been practicing every day with the pistol rig the new deputy had given him. He just didn't know how fast Lupe was learning until one day after Tad could ride, he accompanied his friend down to the creek.

Lupe handed Tad a small stick and asked him to throw it into the creek. He did. Before the stick hit the water Lupe drew, fired, and broke the stick in half. He fired again, and then again, and broke both the floating pieces in half again.

Tad was flabbergasted. He couldn't believe what he had just witnessed. Lupe's hands moved like lightening, drawing and firing faster than the eye could follow.

"How did you do that? I didn't even see you draw, it was so quick."

"Mr. Overstreet is a good teacher. He says I am a natural at handling a pistol."

"Let me show you something else Mr. Hugh taught me," Lupe said, pulling his pistol and carefully removing all the shells, then replacing it in his holster.

"Stand in front of me, up real close, only a step away," Lupe instructed his friend. "Now clap your hands together as fast as you can."

Not understanding what was happening Tad started to clap his hands together, but before his hands met, he discovered the nose of his friend's pistol between them. The pistol had suddenly appeared in his hand like magic. One second he was standing there with his hands by his side, the next instant the weapon was in his hand.

"Holy smoke!" Tad exclaimed. "I didn't even see you draw it was so fast. Could you teach me how to use a pistol like that?"

"I could try. Maybe we could practice together."

"Next time I'm in town I'll buy me a gun rig like yours."

The opportunity came a week later. They needed supplies from town. This time Mary insisted that Lupe ride along.

"Don't worry," Mary told her son. "We'll be all right until you get back. Marilyn and I have a big washing to put out while you two are gone."

His mother gave him a list of things she needed from the store. Sally reminded her brother that she, "shore would like some candy, bubby." All Marilyn asked for was a new hairbrush and hand mirror.

Tad suggested that since he was now riding his pa's big buckskin, that they throw a packsaddle on old Solomon and take the mule rather than drive the wagon.

"We would make better time," Lupe agreed.

Just as a precaution, Tad strapped his pa's saddle scabbard that held the Greener sawed off shotgun and slid his own Henry rifle into the saddle boot.

"Are you expecting trouble?" Lupe wanted to know.

"No, but I wasn't the last time I went into town either and look what happened. Better safe than sorry."

Tad and Lupe rode into Lubbock an hour shy of noon. They reined up in front of the Sheriff's office and stepped down. Hugh Overstreet was just coming out and greeted them with a wide smile.

"Well, if it ain't the Littlejohn boys, morning, Tad, Lupe."

"Morning, Mr. Overstreet," they both said.

"What are you boys doing in town?"

"We rode in to get a few supplies," Tad said, looping the buckskin's reins around the hitching rail. Lupe did likewise with his pinto. "Is Sheriff Paxton in?"

"He walked up the street to talk to the judge. He ought to be back in a few minutes. You boys want to come in and wait for him?"

"Actually, I needed to talk with you too,"

They walked inside. Hugh took a seat behind the desk. Tad and Lupe found chairs and settled into them.

"What can I do for you?"

"I was wondering if you might consider helping me pick out a gun rig like Lupe's."

Hugh studied on it for a moment before he answered.

"Have you talked to your mother about this?"

"I told her I was gonna ask you."

"And what did she say?"

"She said I was might-near grown and had a mind of my own like my pa. She said if I had made up my mind nothing she could say would change it."

Hugh's gaze took the measure of the boy. He was tall for a boy not quite fifteen, near six foot most likely—tall and thin around the waist. But his shoulders were wide and strong. He was a good-looking boy. His quarter Indian blood showed in the high cheekbones, wide-set, coal-black eyes, and unruly hair. It was the eyes that intrigued Hugh, they had a hard-set look, quick, constantly flicking from side to side, Hugh had seen eyes like that before, they were eyes that usually caused men to step aside.

"Then if that's the case, I'd be glad to help you. As a matter of fact, I was looking at the guns over in Mr. Stubblefield's store just yesterday. I think he might have just what you need."

"Reckon we could walk over and take a look?" Tad asked.

"Don't see why not."

Rising, the trio left the sheriff's office and walked down the boardwalk and crossed the street to the store.

"Morning, Deputy, Tad, Lupe," Mr. Stubblefield said, rising up from stacking merchandise on a shelf. "

"Morning, Mr. Stubblefield," Hugh Overstreet greeted. "Tad wants to take a look at one of those pistols I was looking at yesterday."

"Help yourself. You forgot more about gun rigs than I will ever know. If I can be of help just let me know."

Hugh reached into the glass case and withdrew a pistol in a felt-lined, wooden case. He lifted it out and slowly turned it in his hand, openly admiring the weapon.

"This is a .45 caliber 1873 Colt Peacemaker with a seven inch barrel." Hugh opened it to make sure it was empty and then handed it to Tad. "Far as I can tell, that pistol is balanced perfectly. You won't find a better weapon anywhere."

Tad took the pistol, hefted it, surprised at how heavy it was, and stared at it for a long moment. It felt foreign in his hand, not comfortable like his Henry rifle. *It will take some getting use to,* he thought.

"I'm surprised how heavy it is."

"It will take awhile," Hugh told him, "but you'll get use to the weight in no time."

The deputy selected a matching holster and gun belt from a rack and handed it to Tad.

"Buckle that on and see how it fits."

Tad swung the gun belt around his waist and buckled it. Reaching out, Hugh pulled the holster down Tad's leg to the right height.

"That's about where you want to wear it, down low on your lower hip, just like Lupe's there. How does that feel?"

"It feels funny. I've never wore a pistol before."

"Won't take long until it will feel as natural as putting on your boots," Hugh told him.

Tad bought the gun rig along with four boxes of .45 shells; he would need them for practice.

Leaving the store and walking back toward the sheriff's office, Tad felt like everybody they met was staring at the pistol rig on his hip. Sheriff Paxton was coming down the street to meet them.

"Morning fellows," he greeted, his eyes flicking to the pistol on Tad's hip. "I see you bought yourself a new gun rig?"

"Yep, Mr. Overstreet helped me pick it out." Tad slipped the weapon out of its holster and handed it to the sheriff. George looked it over closely.

"That's a fine piece of workmanship. Don't reckon I ever seen better."

They had stopped on the boardwalk outside the sheriff's office.

"Got a piece of news for you, Tad," George said. "I talked to the judge about what you and I discussed. He couldn't see any reason not to authorize a poster on Buck Slade. If you're sure that's what you want to do, I'll have one made up and distributed to all the Sheriff's offices in Texas."

"What will it say on it?"

"Just like we talked about, five hundred dollars reward, dead or alive."

"That's what I want."

A year passed. Tad had his sixteenth birthday. Lupe turned seventeen. During the past year the two friends grew even closer.

They spent at least part of every day down by the creek practicing with their pistols. Just as Hugh Overstreet had predicted, the pistol became as familiar in Tad's hand as his finger.

But as hard as Tad tried, he couldn't hold a candle to the speed and efficiency with which Lupe handled a pistol. His smooth, lightning-fast draw amazed Tad. They often stood facing one another hour after hour, practicing drawing against one another, then hours more firing at floating targets.

During that year, at Mary's insistence, they made the long trip into town in the wagon most every Sunday to attend church. George Paxton now openly sat with Mary during the services. Afterwards, they usually either had a picnic with the Holly's and the Green's if the weather permitted and if not, they ate Sunday lunch in the local restaurant.

Both Tad and Lupe enjoyed and looked forward to those times, partly because it was a welcome break from the week's backbreaking work, but mostly because it gave them a chance to spend time with the Holly sisters. Tad was sweet on Christine Holly.

"She's the prettiest girl I've ever seen," Tad told Lupe on more than one occasion.

"Not any prettier than Cleo," Lupe always shot back.

"Well, they're both pretty," Tad agreed about the two sisters.

Caleb Green was now openly courting Marilyn. He often came by the house and they went for long horseback rides together.

Things seemed to be going well in the Littlejohn valley. They had increased their cattle herd, built another bedroom onto the house, and George Paxton's visits became more frequent.

But Tad's restlessness grew. His obsession with avenging his father's murder got stronger with every passing day. Mary saw it too.

"What am I going to do?" She asked George one evening after supper as they sat in the front porch swing sipping coffee together. "I can see what's happening to him. I catch him standing for an hour at a time, staring off across the mountains. He's going to go, isn't he?"

George heard the desperation in her voice.

"I'm afraid so, Mary. It's eating him alive. The boy won't rest until he's done what he's set his mind to do."

"I know. He's just like his father. Once his mind's made up nothing on God's green earth will change it. I had hoped he would forget it and let it lie but I'm afraid that's not going to happen."

"No, I'm afraid it's not."

"But what would I do if..." She couldn't bear to think the thought, let alone say it. "I lost T.J. I don't think I could bear losing my son too."

Mary swallowed hard, trying to dislodge the knot that stuck in her throat. Tears breached her eyelids and traced down her cheeks. A sob worked its way past the knot and erupted as a heartbreaking cry, jolting her body. George encircled her shaking shoulders with an arm and drew her close. She buried her face in the hollow of his shoulder and wept uncontrollably.

Finally Mary's sobbing subsided. Silence lengthened. Shep lay curled on the porch beside them. A whip-o-will called in the night. A cow bellowed. The night played its symphony of sound.

The time Mary had dreaded arrived a few mornings later. She somehow sensed it was about to happen. Tad sat at the breakfast table, staring at his untouched cup of coffee, lost in his own thought.

"Ma, there's something I need to talk with you about," he said without looking up.

Her son's words shredded Mary's heart, hitting her like a sledgehammer. A feeling of mounting panic swept over her, consuming her, drowning her in confusion and dread.

She swung a look at her son. His eyes rose to meet hers. She stared into the innocent face of her sixteen year old son, and saw instead the face of a mature man, a man consumed with a fire in his soul that would never be quenched until he had avenged his father's death.

"I know, son, I know," Mary whispered, barely choking the words out. "But avenging your father's death won't bring him back."

"I've got it to do, Ma, it just won't let go of me."

"Please, son," Mary choked out desperately. "Please don't do this. I couldn't bear to lose you too."

"Ma, you know I'd do anything you asked me to do, but please don't ask me not to go. It's eating me alive, ma. I've got to go."

"I don't want you to go, son, God in Heaven knows I don't, but you're just like your pa, and I know you feel you have to. Will Lupe be going with you?"

Tad gave a single nod.

"I talked to Homer Green the other day. He said he's going to have to lay his hired hand off for awhile. You remember Ray Sawyer. I'd like to hire him to take care of things while we're gone if that's all right with you?"

"If that's what you think best."

"I thought we could clean out the tack room in the barn for him to sleep in."

"That will be fine. When will you be leaving?"

"Soon as I can get things together, most likely tomorrow."

# Chapter VII

A thick grayness of early morning tinged the eastern horizon. It was barely daylight. Tad's big buckskin and Lupe's black and white pinto were saddled and cinched. Their bedrolls, rain slickers, and long canvas dusters were tied behind their saddles.

Both boys wore tied-down pistols and had their Henry rifles riding backwards in saddle boots. Tad also carried two ten-gauge Greener shotguns sawed off to twenty-six inch barrels.

Solomon, their pack mule, stood nearby with his packs mostly empty except for T. J.'s old trail utensils, cooking pans and coffee pot. Tad meant to pick up their trail supplies as they rode through Lubbock.

Mary had baked two dozen fried apple pies which Tad wrapped in a white cloth and packed into one of his saddle bags.

They were all gathered near the corral to say their goodbyes. Everyone present was on the verge of tears.

Little Sally broke the uneasy silence by running into her brother's arms.

"Goodbye, bubby, I'll miss you."

"I'll miss you too. You be good and mind your mother."

Marilyn stepped forward then. She first hugged Lupe, and then her brother.

"Be careful, Tad, and hurry back to us."

"We'll be back before you know it, sis."

With a turn of his head, Tad stared at his mother. Mary stood with her head bowed, staring at her feet, clearly struggling to retain her composure. Large tears betrayed her and scored hot trails down her cheeks. She bit her lower lip the way she always did when she was upset.

Tad opened his arms. Mary allowed a small cry to escape her lips and rushed into her son's arms. All the pent up emotions burst the dam and flooded forth. She buried her face in Tad's long, unruly, black hair, crying openly. He held her for several long minutes. Mother and son embraced, perhaps for the last time.

"I love you, ma," Tad chocked out. "I love you more than life. But this is something I have to do. I can't live with myself or anyone else until I get it done."

Mary couldn't speak. The words just wouldn't come out. She lifted her tear-stained face and stared long into her son's dark eyes, his father's eyes. She shook a single nod and turned away, burying her face in her wadded-up apron.

Tad and Lupe rode into Lubbock just shy of noon. They reined their horses to a stop in front of Mr. Stubblefield's store and swung from their mounts to the dusty street. The storekeeper was sweeping the boardwalk in front of his store.

"Morning Tad, Lupe, you boys look like you're packed for a trip."

"Morning, Mr. Stubblefield. We'll be needing enough trail supplies for a couple of weeks."

"Where you boys heading?"

"Riding over to New Mexico Territory."

"Figured as much. Most of us had a notion that would be coming one of these days. Come on in, boys, we'll get you outfitted."

The storekeeper busied himself gathering up the pile of supplies Tad and Lupe would need. Tad watched the stack of stuff grow steadily larger and wondered if they could possibly get all that onto Solomon's packs.

George and Hugh walked in just as Mr. Stubblefield finished and was figuring up their bill.

"Guess I don't have to ask where you boys are headed."

"It's time," Tad said.

"Don't reckon there's any way I can talk you out of this?"

Tad just shook his head once. "I got it to do Mr. Paxton, putting it off won't make it any easier."

Hugh stood silently nearby, staring at the two boys. Finally, he walked over to Tad and Lupe and looked them straight in the eyes.

"Want some company?"

They all jerked a questioning look at the deputy.

"What do you mean?" Tad asked.

"I'd like to ride along if you boys have no objections."

Hugh swung a look at the sheriff.

"George, I've been thinking on this for awhile. Things are pretty quiet around here right now and I need some time off. I think a little ride down New Mexico way would do me good. What do you say?"

"If that's what you want to do, take all the time you need."

"Well boys," Hugh Overstreet said. "You heard the sheriff, now it's up to you, Mind if I ride along?"

"Be right proud to have you, Mr. Overstreet," Tad said. "Mr. Paxton, we've hired Ray Sawyer to help take care of things around the place while we've gone, but I sure would be obliged if you'd look in on ma and the girls from time to time."

"I'll look after them, son. You've got my word on it."

The afternoon was half-spent before Hugh Overstreet could make arrangements for a packhorse and get his things together. The trio pulled out of Lubbock and headed their horses into the sun.

"If we hurry these horses, boys, we can make the Sulphur Draw of the Colorado River not long after dark," Hugh said. "I thought that might be a good place to make camp for the night. What do you think?"

"Sounds good to me," Tad replied.

Tad's stomach was a mish-mash of emotions: excitement, anticipation, apprehension, fear, not knowing what to expect, concern for his mother and sisters at home. All these feelings and more made his stomach queasy and his head spin.

He was glad that Lupe and Hugh Overstreet were along. The thought that he had figured to make the trip by himself now scared him to death and he began to realize what an impossible trip it would have been alone.

They rode at a ground-eating pace, alternating between a short-lope and a fast walk. Their horses were rested and seemed full of energy.

The country was as flat as the top of their kitchen table at home. One could see for miles in any direction. There were no trees except for a few clusters of stunted mesquite here and there. The soil was reddish-brown clay that was cooked under the brutal sun and cracked. There were large patches of gray-white caliche.

Grass was sparse, and had a yellowish color with silver tassels. Tad had heard some of the old timers call it Mule Weed. It stood knee-high to the horses and swayed in the strong, hot wind like ripples on the water when a stone is tossed into it.

"They call this area the Llano Estacado or High Plain. Some call it the Staked Plains," Hugh told the boys. "It's real easy to lose your sense of direction since there are no mountains and very few trees. Wagon trains that come through here sometimes drive stakes in the ground to keep track of their direction. They point the tongue of their wagons toward the North Star at night so they will know what direction to head out the next morning.

"We're making good time. If we can keep up this pace we ought to reach the river by good dark."

"Sounds like you've been through here before," Tad said.

"Oh yeah, there ain't many places I haven't been in the last several years. I've moved around a lot.

"Lupe, when you and Tad's pa rode through here, did you come this way?"

"Not sure. It all looks the same."

"Yeah, it does don't it?"

Darkness was just settling in when the trio reined up on the bank of the Colorado River. After watering their horses, they found a deep arroyo with a few gnarled mesquite bushes and made camp.

After a good meal cooked over the campfire, they settled down with a cup of coffee and some of Mary's fried pies to relax for a few minutes before turning in.

The full moon was so bright one could see his own shadow. Scrub mesquites made dark skeletons against the night sky. Tall barrel cactus, some taller than a man's head, stood like silent sentries and cast eerie shadows in the desert night. Off in the distance, a coyote called to its mate. It was a lonely sound.

The sound of gurgling water jerked Tad awake from a sound sleep. He blinked his eyes open to a gray dawn. Hugh was squatting near the fire pouring water from his canteen into a blackened coffee pot.

A strong wind from the west gathered sand into a swirling cloud and drove the gray mass before it. The stinging particles bit into their skin and saturated everything in its path. Tad shielded his eyes against the blowing sand and pulled his bandana up over his nose and mouth.

"Looks like we're in for a blow," Hugh said quietly.

"I'd say," Tad answered.

He shook out his boots and pulled them on, then woke Lupe.

"What say we make do on a cup of coffee for breakfast? All that sand in my food don't do nothing for my appetite," Hugh asked.

Both boys agreed and in less than a half-hour they had broke camp, watered the horses, shouldered into their long canvas dusters, and were in the saddle.

They rode steady, bowing their heads into the howling sandstorm, picking their way across the flat desert-like plains. By mid-afternoon they crossed the Sulphur Springs branch of the River where they watered their stock and hunkered down in a draw to take a break from the wind.

"I figure we'll cross into New Mexico Territory sometime before noon tomorrow," Hugh told them.

"Is it flat like this all the way to where we're going?" Tad asked.

"No, it gets much rougher as we get further into New Mexico," Lupe told him.

"Yeah," Hugh agreed. "This is the easy part. We need to fill our extra canteens. We'll likely have a dry camp tonight. May not find water for a couple of days."

Hugh Overstreet was right, it was two thirsty days later before they found water. A small stream threaded along the bottom of a narrow, rocky canyon. The water was muddy-looking but neither the horses nor men seemed to mind, they drank it like it was pure and crystal clear.

They took time to shuck their clothes and bathe. The water was almost hot, but felt good and left them refreshed. Hugh insisted that only two of them bathe at once and that their rifles be kept handy.

"We're getting deep into Apache country, boys," he said. "We best keep our eyes peeled just in case. What do you think about making an early camp? There's still another three or four hours daylight but I think this might be a good place to rest up a little. The horses could use a blow too. Let's set up our camp over there between those two large boulders."

They all agreed.

Unknown to them, other eyes watched as the trio busied themselves setting up their camp for the night. Soon, darkness enveloped the land.

The new hired hand was filling both wooden water barrels from the creek when George Paxton splashed his dappled-gray gelding downstream and crossed the creek.

He reined up and swung to the ground, dropping his reins to ground hitch his mount.

"Afternoon, Ray."

"Afternoon, Sheriff."

"How's your new job working out?"

"Couldn't be better. Mrs. Littlejohn is a fine woman. She shore sets a mighty good table too."

"Don't I know it? I rode out this afternoon hoping I would get an invite to supper."

"I'm thinking we might have fried chicken. I saw her wringing a young fryer's neck awhile ago."

Ray Sawyer placed the lids on the water barrels and scotched them down tight so the water wouldn't slosh out. Then climbed into the wagon seat and took up the reins to the team of mules.

"Ray, have you seen any sign of Indians in the last couple of days?"

"No, don't reckon I have. Is there something I ought to know?"

"Most likely nothing but I got a telegram saying some renegade Comanche raided an isolated farm a hundred miles north. They think they're headed this direction. Don't say anything. No use worrying Mrs. Littlejohn without need. You might want to keep that rifle within easy reach just in case. When you get over to the house I'll help you unload them barrels." George told the hired hand.

"I'm obliged."

George toed a stirrup and swung into his saddle and gigged his mount toward the cabin. Little Sally saw him coming from her tree swing and ran to meet him.

"Hey, Mr. Paxton. You gonna stay for supper? Please, pretty please? We could play checkers. "

"Well, do you reckon I could talk your mother into asking me? My stomach tells me you're having fried chicken?"

"How'd you know that?" She said with a puzzled look on her pretty face.

"Why, didn't you know? Men folk can always tell when women are fixing fried chicken for supper."

"Mr. Paxton, you're just teasing me."

"Good afternoon, George," Mary called from the door.

George Paxton swung a look. She was standing there wiping flour from her hands onto the apron she wore around her waist. Her flour-sack, flowery work dress made her look like she was dressed for a church picnic. Her hair hung loose about her shoulders and captured the fading sun, crowning her head with a halo of a thousand golden candles glinting in her hair. He walked toward her with his long-gaited strides.

"I swear to my time, Mary, if you don't get prettier every time I ride out here."

"I bet you say that to all the women you eat supper with."

"Was that an invitation to supper? If so, I accept."

"We're just having fried chicken."

"You know that's my favorite."

"Why do you think I fixed it?" She smiled. "Have a seat on the porch, I'll bring you a cup of coffee."

George scooted the rocking chair around and folded into it. He watched the hired hand pulling the wagon toward the house.

"How's Ray Sawyer working out?" He called over his shoulder.

"Just fine. He's a good worker. He knows what needs to be done and does it without being told. He's about to eat me out of house and home though," she laughed. "He can eat more than any man I know, except you, of course."

"Well, it's your fault. You shouldn't be such a good cook."

Ray backed the wagon up to the front porch and the two men unloaded the barrels of water. Mary brought George a cup of coffee and the hired hand took the wagon to unhitch the mules and do the evening chores.

"I promised Sally I'd play her some checkers after supper."

"You're spoiling that girl rotten."

"That's what children are for."

"You like children don't you?"

"I love children. Always wanted a family, just never worked out. How can you tell?"

"Women can just tell about those things."

"What else can women tell about a man?"

Well...maybe that's a subject we better talk about another time. I think I better go check on supper."

After supper and a half-dozen games of checkers, all of which Sally won, of course, George pushed up from the table.

"Reckon I better be heading back toward town, it's a long ride."

"It's too late for you to ride back tonight, George. Why don't you wait until morning? I could fix you a pallet on the floor."

"Well, it is late. If it's okay, I'll just bed down in the barn?"

"Of course it would be okay, but you're welcome to sleep in the house."

"The barn will be fine. Goodnight, folks."

"Breakfast will be ready by sunup," Mary said.

"I'll be looking forward to it."

Sally had long since said goodnight and headed to her bedroom. Marilyn said her goodnights and left George and Mary alone. As George headed for the door Mary followed and walked out onto the porch.

"Thanks for a wonderful supper," George said.

"You're very welcome."

George turned to go. Mary's soft, hesitant voice behind him stopped him in his tracks.

"George. It's such a pretty evening. Could we sit awhile?"

"I'd like that."

They sat down side-by-side on the edge of the porch. For long minutes they stared up at the velvety night sky. Twinkling stars sparkled like diamonds against the velvety black background. The poignant sweetness of pine drifted on a soft breeze.

"Mind if I ask you a question?" She asked hesitantly.

"Of course. You can ask me anything."

"How long did it take you to get over losing your wife?"

He thought on her question for a long minute before answering.

"In some ways, I reckon I still haven't got over it. Somebody said that time is the great healer. That may be so—it helps, sure enough. I don't think about her as much as I did for awhile."

"Do you still love her?"

"I'll always love her."

"Do you think you could ever love someone else?"

The question shocked George. He didn't know how to answer. *Is she asking what it sounds like she's asking?* He wondered. Her question gave birth to a spark of hope deep inside him.

He swung a slow look at her. She was looking at him. Their eyes met. Something beyond words passed between them, something that sent a surge of hope rushing over him.

"Yes," he answered simply. "Could you?"

"I don't know, George. I honestly don't know...maybe in time."


It wasn't what he heard, it was what he didn't hear that woke

Hugh Overstreet from a sound sleep. The ever-present night birds and tree locust, whose constant chatter filled the night unless disturbed, were suddenly silent. His worst fear was confirmed when Solomon, their pack mule, let out a low, rumbling snort deep inside his chest and swung a stare at a clump of nearby willow trees. They had uninvited company.

Careful to move nothing but his hand, he snaked his rifle underneath his blanket and levered a shell into the chamber.

Tad must have heard the pack mule too and reached a hand to wake Lupe. Hugh heard both jack shells into their rifles as well as the familiar double-click of Tad's shotgun being cocked.

"Quick, get behind those rocks," Hugh whispered, even as he threw himself into a roll to his left and came to crouch, his rifle aimed into the thick darkness.

The soft swish of arrows pierced the night. Hugh saw two of the messengers of death plunge deep into the bedroll he had just vacated. Both Tad and Lupe were beside him.

A thin moon revealed vague shadows charging toward them from every direction. Hugh fired, levered another shell and fired again. The rattle of gunfire beside him told him Tad and Lupe had also found targets.

A muffled cry came from somewhere in front of Hugh and a body fell headlong at his feet. A shotgun blast to his left jarred the night and blew another running Indian over backwards. A shadow moved to his right. He swung the nose of his rifle and fired pointblank. A blood-curdling scream told him his aim had been true.

As quickly as the battle had started, it ended. The Apache simply disappeared into the night like a vapor.

"Is anyone hurt?" Hugh asked anxiously.

"I'm okay," Tad answered with a shaky breath.

"So am I," Lupe replied.

"Stay hunkered down. We were lucky this time. They may come at us again."

They waited.

# Chapter VIII

George Paxton lay on his back in the soft, sweet-smelling hay in the loft of the barn. His hands were laced behind his head and a booted foot was propped on an upraised knee. He stared through the dim darkness at the sheet-iron roof, replaying the evening's events and half expecting to wake up and discover it had all been nothing more than a wonderful dream.

Mary Littlejohn was everything he had ever dreamed of and more than he could have hoped for. She was beautiful and smart and she stirred feelings inside him he thought were long dead.

He had answered Mary's question honestly. He loved his late wife and always would, but the feelings he now felt for Mary were different, fresh, exciting. He felt like a young schoolboy. He dared not reveal to Mary his true feelings, at least not yet.

Ray's loud snoring from below blended with sounds from the farm animals to disturb the quietness of the night. Shep slept just inside the double-door of the barn allowing George to relax in the knowledge that the dog would alert him if any intruder came near.

The night was mostly spent before George finally fell asleep. It was a contented sleep.

A rooster announced the birth of a new day and jolted George awake. Dawn had already settled across the land and he'd overslept. Shaking out his boots, he pulled them on and hurriedly climbed down the ladder from the hayloft.

The hired hand was forking hay to the two horses and two mules in the corral when George emerged from the barn. Smoke from Mary's breakfast fire trailed upward from the stovepipe and bent sharply on a soft, westerly breeze. George angled toward the corral.

Shep trotted to meet him but suddenly stopped, swung a look toward the creek, and let out a deep, rumbling growl. George peered through the early morning twilight. What he saw brought his heart into his throat.

Near a dozen mounted Indians were wading their horses across the creek and were headed toward the house. No doubt about it, it was the band of renegade Comanche George had been warned about.

"Ray, drop everything and grab your rifle, quick, take cover in the barn, we've got company coming."

George broke into a long-legged trot toward the house. Mounting the porch with a single leap he slammed open the front door. Mary jerked around and pinned him with a questioning look.

"Close the shutters, Mary, hurry, Indians coming."

Grabbing the shotgun that hung over the front door he dumped a box of double-aught shells on the table and thumbed two shells into the twin barrels. Laying it on the table he withdrew his .44 and spun the cylinder to make sure it was fully loaded.

Mary and Marilyn were running through the house closing and barring the heavy shutters.

Thumbing back both hammers, he cradled the shotgun in the crook of his arm and walked to the front door and stepped outside. The Comanche were walking their horses toward the house. They reined to a stop twenty yards from the front.

There were seven Indians, but only six horses; two rode double. The ponies were all scrawny, slat-ribbed animals that looked half-starved.

The obvious leader walked his brown and white pinto forward. He was tall for a Comanche, tall and broad-shouldered. His coal-black hair hung loose below his shoulders, held in place by a strip of leather across his forehead. A single eagle feather was knotted in the tangled mass of hair.

His chest was bare but he wore long deerskin leggings covered by a breach clout. His dark eyes darted to and fro, searching for any sign of danger. An older model Henry rifle was propped upright on one leg held by the renegade's right hand.

George had fought the Comanche on several occasions over the years. He recognized the dress and markings as Kwadies, the fiercest and most blood thirsty tribe in the west.

He had witnessed their handiwork many times. Their unmistakable trademark was all too familiar along the Texas-New Mexico frontier. They tied down the men and children, slit their bellies open and scattered their intestines in the dirt while they were still alive. It was the most painful death anyone could imagine. The women were repeatedly raped, and then their throats were slit and left to bleed to death.

"You speak English?" George asked, meeting the leader's hard stare with one of his own.

George saw two of the renegades turn their ponies and head toward the corral where George's steel-gray gelding and Tad's sorrel stood.

"I speak," the man replied, pointing with his head toward the corral. "We take horses."

"No," George said firmly, his stare never wavering from the Indian's eyes.

A surprised look swept across the renegade leader's face.

"If either of your men touches that corral gate I'll kill you."

The words came out hard as iron. As he spoke he swung the shotgun from the crook of his arm and leveled it hip-high, square on the leader.

"Now turn your horses around and git while you still can."

The renegade hesitated. George felt his palm get suddenly sweaty. He drew in a long breath and held it, waiting for what he knew was coming.

He knew the Comanche wouldn't just ride away. They would fight, but they would fight on their own terms. George had the drop on the tall leader and the Indian knew it. He would turn and pretend to ride away, and then when he got out of shotgun range he would wheel and use the rifle in his hand. George cursed himself for bringing the shotgun instead of his Winchester rifle.

Sure enough, the leader kneed his pinto around just as George had thought he would. *I can't let him ride away,* he thought.

George nudged the trigger of his shotgun. A thundering explosion accompanied the drop of the hammer and rocked the morning stillness. Buckshot riddled the bronzed skin of the renegade's back. The tall Comanche was torn completely off his horse by the force of the double-aught buckshot, his back riddled with countless wounds. A shrill cry burst from the Indian's throat, outlasting the dying roar of the shotgun.

"Mary! Toss me my rifle!" George shouted.

From the barn, Ray opened up on the two Comanche near the corral gate. His first shot hit the renegade square in the chest. The rider flew from the back of his pony, dead before he hit the ground.

Ray's second shot hit the other Indian in the stomach, badly wounding him. The man slumped over the neck of his horse and kicked it into a gallop.

Mary was at the door and quickly handed George his Winchester. He levered a shell and brought it to his shoulder. Sighting along the long barrel he laid the sights on the back of a fleeing Indian and feathered the trigger.

Before he looked to see the results of his shot, he worked the lever and swung the nose to find another target.

A Comanche arched his back and hurried a hand to the new hole that appeared there before tumbling from his pony.

George found another target, though a small one. The two remaining renegades were lying near flat on the sides of their galloping ponies. One leg draped over the horse's back allowed them to make themselves a near impossible target.

The Comanche were widely known as the fiercest fighters and the best horseman the world had ever known, George was getting a demonstration of why.

He took a deep breath, let it out, and adjusted the nose of his rifle to line up his shot. It was a long shot and his target was becoming fuzzy from his failing eyesight. He gently squeezed the trigger.

Off in the distance, approaching the trees along the creek, a Comanche slid from his running horse and tumbled along the ground. George let out a long slide of air and lowered his Winchester.

* * *

It seemed the night would never pass. A thin slice of silver moonlight paled the darkness. Hugh, Tad, and Lupe tensed at every sound. They peered into the blackness until their eyes burned. Nothing disturbed the natural sounds.

False dawn grayed the east. Another hour would creep by before the sun would awaken. Morning crept slowly into the little canyon where they waited anxiously for the second attack that never came. Finally convinced that the Apache were not returning, they rose cautiously and began breaking camp.

By sun-up they had fed and watered their stock and finished a hurried breakfast. They wanted to put as many tracks between them and their attackers as possible.

They mounted up and kept their rifles in hand as they rode out. Hugh took the lead with Tad watching their back trail.

As the miles passed underneath their horses, the mid-morning sun baked into them, rendering the desert-like terrain scorching hot, even the lizards and desert mice scurried from shade to shade, anxious to escape the heat.

The country through which they traveled lay along a river, Lupe said it was called the Rio Penasco River. The area was dotted with scrub mesquite, ocotillo and deep arroyos that scared the landscape. Red, rocky peaks jutted toward the blue sky. Large fields of cactus beds caused frequent detours in order to avoid the needle-sharp spines. This was a no-man's land where even the hardiest of creatures struggled to survive. Only those who had seen it for themselves understood how harsh, how empty, how deadly it could be.

The creak of saddle leather and the rattle of shod hooves against the ever-present rocks, accompanied them down a twisting, shallow, ravine that opened to a brush-choked flat. Hugh watched numerous birds head in that direction and suspected they would find a waterhole there. Both men and horses were exhausted, their strength sapped away by the unrelenting heat.

His suspicions were correct. A small spring bubbled out from under a rocky ledge and formed an inviting pool of clear, fresh water. Leaning in his saddle, he inspected the tracks surrounding the area. Tracks of unshod ponies showed clearly but were not fresh; it had been days since anyone visited the spring.

"We'll fill our canteens and water the horses. That outcropping over yonder looks like a good place to bed down for the night," Hugh told his two companions.

Camped below the ledge with a full view on three sides and several large boulders in front of them, it would be an easy place to defend should they have visitors during the night. Ashes from old campfires gave witness that others had used this shelter before.

They scooped out a shallow hole to minimize the fire being seen and built a small fire, made coffee, and warmed a jar of beans and salt pork for supper.

After supper, as they had every night, they spent an hour practicing drawing their pistols and being schooled in the art of gun fighting. After the session they sat around the campfire for a spell before turning in.

"How far you reckon we are from Alamogordo?" Hugh asked after a sip of coffee.

Lupe lifted his gaze off to the west in contemplation before answering.

"Hard to say, another couple of days maybe. Those mountains off to the west would be the Sacramento Range. Mr.

Littlejohn and I crossed them when we came through here. You ever been to New Mexico before?"

"Yeah, rode through Santa Fe once on my way to Colorado, but it's been awhile."

"You never talk much about yourself, Mr. Hugh. Mind me asking where you're from?" Tad asked.

"Not much to talk about," Hugh said, staring into the fire. "I was born in Alabama. My parents moved to south Texas when I was a little tad. We farmed a patch of dirt and raised a few cattle.

"Married the prettiest girl in Texas and settled down on a little spread a few miles south of San Antonio. The Big Man upstairs blessed us with an angel named Hannah. She was prettier than a ray of morning sunshine."

For a long minute, then two, the gunfighter, turned lawman, sipped his coffee and stared absently into the campfire. When he finally spoke again his voice had taken on a firmness neither of the boys had heard before. Cold. Hard. Unyielding.

"I was out rounding up strays from my little herd of cattle. They came. There were six of them. They took turns with my wife and nine year old daughter. When they finished, they murdered them both.

"When I got home and found them I buried my family, burned the house and barn, and went after them. It took me three years. I hunted down every last one of them.

"By the time it was over I had a reputation as a gunfighter. I never wanted it, never went looking for it, it just sorta happened, I reckon. Every two-bit gunman wanted a piece of me. They somehow thought if they could gun me down they would become a big man, the fastest gun around.

"I drifted for several years, trying to run away from my own shadow. But everywhere I went there was always somebody willing to die to have what I didn't want, a reputation as the fastest gunfighter alive.

"Sheriff Paxton gave me a chance to change all that. Then I met the two of you, and here I am. End of story."

"What made you decide to come with us, Mr. Overstreet?" Lupe asked.

Again, the gunfighter sipped his coffee and thought about the question. His answer was a long time coming.

"Hard question. Don't rightly know if I even know the whole answer. If the Man upstairs keeps a book like everybody says, Lord knows I got enough bad written down on the wrong side of His ledger, guess I saw a chance to put something good on the other side.

"Guess everybody wants their life to count for something. I ain't got much in that department I can point to. We'll get your man, Tad, or die trying. I reckon the Good Lord might see fit to write that down on the good side of the book."

# Chapter IX

They rode into town from the south. Shadows of twilight were lengthening. The single dusty street of Alamogordo was mostly deserted. Only three saddled horses stood hipshot in front of the rundown saloon.

The three travelers were a pitiful sight. Tired, hungry, their long dusters caked with dust, they looked like three castaways from the desert. They reined their little caravan of sweat-soaked horses toward the ram-shackled livery stable.

Hugh Overstreet swung his leg over the saddle and lowered himself stiffly to the ground. They had been in the saddle from sunup until dark for more than a week. *I'm getting too old for this*, he thought, as he stamped feeling back into his feet.

An elderly, stooped Mexican limped tiredly from the darkening interior of the livery stable.

"Howdy, strangers. Looks like you fellows have come a ways."

"A ways" Hugh said, stamping his feet to get the circulation going.

The old hostler took a few steps toward them before stopping abruptly in his tracks. His tired eyes squinted at the three strangers for a long breath of time.

Lupe leaped from his saddle and bounded the few steps that separated him from the old liveryman.

"*Madre de Dios!*" The old man shouted. "*Lupe,* my son, is it you?"

"*Si,* Mr. Lopez. It is me. It's good to see you again."

"But you have grown into a man in this short time, and a handsome one to boot. Why have you returned to Alamogordo?"

"We have come on a mission, Señor *Lopez.* These are my friends. This is Mr. Hugh Overstreet and this is Tad Littlejohn. He is the son of our friend, Mr. T.J. Littlejohn. Mr. Littlejohn was murdered, shot in the back by Buck Slade."

"*Si*, he has bragged for two years of killing your father, but he told that it was in a fair fight. I never believed it."

"Is Señor Short still the marshal in Alamogordo?" Lupe asked.

"*Si.*"

"We'll need our horses cared for," Hugh Overstreet said. "Double rations of oats, rub them down good, and stall them with plenty of water and hay. We'll be over at the hotel for awhile."

"As you wish, *señor,*" the old hostler said, gathering the reins. "I see you're still riding that pinto the town gave you. I remember this big buckskin and that ornery Missouri Mule too."

"I'll stop by and we'll catch up on all that's been going on for the last couple of years," Lupe told his old friend.

"That will be a happy day," the old timer said.

After checking into the small hotel, they all agreed what they wanted most was a good meal, a hot bath, and a soft bed.

They made arrangements with the desk clerk for the hot bath to be ready as soon as they returned from supper.

Sadie's place was everything Lupe had told them it would be, small, clean, with good food. Sadie greeted them warmly, then, after recognizing Lupe, gathered him into her big arms and smothered him to her large breasts.

Finally released from her bear hug, Lupe introduced his friends to the friendly restaurant owner and told her what had happened to T.J.

"Right sorry to hear about your pa," she told Tad. "The first time I met him I could tell right off he was a good man. About all he talked about was his family back home. I ain't surprised to hear Buck Slade shot him in the back, either. That's the kind of man he is. He rides around on that big, black horse acting like a big man, but I got him pegged as a coward."

"What you got back there that's hot and filling?" Hugh asked.

"Beef stew with potatoes and onions. Hot and spicy and guaranteed to put hairs on your chest."

That broke a grin.

"Reckon these two youngsters could use some of those, sure enough. Bring us three bowls. You got corn bread?"

"Does Texas have cows? I bake the best corn bread you ever put in your mouth."

Sadie wasn't lying. All three of them ate until they couldn't hold another bite. At least they thought so until she brought out a big slice of apple pie apiece. Somehow they all managed to find room for that.

"I'm so full I ain't sure I can walk back to the hotel," Hugh told his two friends as they climbed out of their chairs.

"See you fellows bright and early for breakfast," Miss Sadie called, as they pushed out the door.

\* \* \*

Lying in the dark hotel room after a good, hot bath, Tad was lost in memories of home.

Leaving home had been, without a doubt, the hardest thing he had ever had to do. But he knew it must have been doubly hard on his mother. He sure did miss the family.

He was well aware that his chances of coming out of this alive were slim to none. The odds of success were almost beyond belief. But he also knew that he had no choice. This was something he simply had to do.

Slanting a glance, he watched Lupe's sleeping form beside him.

*I've never had a friend like Lupe. He's more than a friend. He's like the brother I always wished for. I know why he came with me. He's planning on killing Buck Slade before Slade can kill me. I can't let that happen. I've got to be the one to avenge my father's death.*

His thoughts drifted. Sleep wrapped its arms around him.

The morning sun was peeking over the eastern horizon and lighting the faces of the buildings when the three newcomers to Alamogordo strode up the dusty street toward Sadie's café. The town was waking up. Somewhere a rooster crowed. A dog barked. A heavy freight wagon pulled by a double team rumbled past. The grisly old teamster spat a stream of tobacco juice and nodded a howdy.

"After breakfast, we need to stop by and have a talk with that marshal friend of yours," Hugh told Lupe.

"I figure he's already heard we are in town," Lupe told him. "Not much goes on in this town that he don't know about."

They pushed through the door to Sadie's. Two of the tables

were already occupied. A drummer in an oversized business suit and bowler hat was sipping coffee and reading a newspaper at one of the tables. Four tough-looking cowboy-types nursed coffee at the other table. Everyone in the small room turned to stare when the newcomers walked in.

Hugh and his companions headed for a table near the back wall and were pulling out chairs when Sadie came in from the kitchen carrying a big, blackened coffee pot.

"Morning, Gents," she welcomed, as she poured three cups of steaming, black coffee. "What you fellas gonna have this morning?"

"Give me three eggs, bacon, and a pan of biscuits," Hugh told her.

"I'll have the same," Tad said.

"Me too," Lupe agreed.

Hugh blew the steam away from his coffee and chanced a sip.

"You boys strangers in town, aren't you?" One of the cowboys said from a nearby table.

"Just passing through," Hugh replied, swinging a glance at the speaker.

He was a big fellow, at least a head taller than his three companions, even sitting down. His shoulders were the width of a double tree and his arms as big as a normal man's leg. Clearly, he was not a man one would want to make mad.

His three partners were obvious working cowboys. All four wore tied down pistols.

"Alamogordo ain't a place you just happen to pass through. A fellow about has to come here on purpose," the big cowboy said.

Hugh turned his attention back to his coffee, ignoring the fellow's comment.

"Hey, Mex, you look familiar. Ain't you the kid that use to hang around here a couple years ago?"

Lupe flicked a glance at Hugh, then at the speaker.

"I lived here," Lupe said evenly.

"Yeah, I remember you. You're the little greaser that caused all that trouble with Billy Slade a couple years back."

"Look, mister, we don't want any trouble," Hugh told the loudmouth. "Leave the kid alone."

"I ain't talking to you, old man."

"But I'm talking to you," Hugh said. "You'd be wise to drop it."

The loudmouth jumped from his chair, turning it over. He stalked across the room, brushing chairs and a table aside as he came.

"Nobody tells me what to do!" he bellowed as he approached Hugh Overstreet with his huge fists knotted.

Rising calmly from his chair with his cup of coffee still in his hand, Hugh turned to face the oncoming giant. The big man swung a vicious haymaker that, had it landed, would have torn a man's head off. Hugh stepped aside with the ease and swiftness of a bullfighter, allowing the man to rush by. As the bully charged past, Hugh emptied the steaming coffee into the man's face.

The giant screamed like a wounded grizzly. His hands flew to his face. In the blink of an eye, Hugh drew his Smith & Wesson and struck the troublemaker over his right ear, dropping him like a sack of potatoes. Without stopping his motion, he swung his pistol to cover the big man's companions, who were still in the motion of leaping from their chairs.

"I wouldn't," he told them.

They eased back down into their chairs with their hands well away from their pistols.

In all the excitement, no one had noticed when Marshal Short opened the door and stepped inside, until he spoke.

"Nice work, whoever you might be."

"I'm Hugh Overstreet. You must be the Marshal."

The lawman walked over to the table where the three cowboys sat and held out his hand.

"Maybe you boys better let me keep those hog legs for you for a few days, just to make sure this little disagreement ends right here. Do we understand one another? Now pick up your partner and douse his head in the water trough outside and get him back to the ranch."

The three cowboys handed the marshal their pistols and picked up their partner. The marshal lifted the unconscious man's pistol from his holster as they dragged him out the door. Only then did he turn to face Hugh and the two boys.

"I'm Marshal Tom Short. Did I hear you say your name is Hugh Overstreet? You from down Texas way by chance?"

"I've been there."

"Uh-huh. I know the name. You're the Texas gun fighter that gunned down the three Turley brothers down in Abilene a year or so back. The way I heard it they drew first and you killed all three before their pistols cleared leather. News like that travels far and fast."

"They needed killing."

"Lupe, it's good to see you again. You're riding in pretty fast company," the marshal said. "What brings you back to Alamogordo?"

"I've got some unfinished business."

"Wouldn't have anything to do with that friend of yours, T.J.Littlejohn getting shot, would it?"

"Marshal, my name is Tad Littlejohn." Tad spoke up. "T. J. was my pa. Buck Slade shot him in the back. I've got a warrant for his arrest and a wanted poster that says, dead or alive. I mean to see he's brought to justice."

"I ain't seen no warrant or poster like that," the marshal said. "I met your pa when he was here looking to collect bounty on the *Sanchez* brothers awhile back. Toughest hombre I ever laid eyes on."

Tad pulled the documents from his pocket and handed them to Marshal Short. He studied them for several long minutes.

"They seem to be in order, sure enough," he admitted, handing them back to Tad. "Trouble is, anybody that tries to serve that warrant will end up buzzard bait. Buck Slade's got fifty or more hard cases riding for him. You just met four of them. One of his hired hands is Ace Bonham. That name might not mean anything to you boys, but I'd wager Mr. Overstreet knows the name."

"Yeah," Hugh said, "I know the name."

"I'm sorry about your pa," the lawman told Tad. "He was a good man. Fact is I liked him. Slade admits he killed your pa, fact is, he brags about it, but his story is he shot him in a face to face, stand up fair fight."

"That's a lie!" Tad said angrily.

"Figured it was, but that don't change the situation here. It would take an army to serve that warrant. Besides that, his ranch is out of my jurisdiction."

"It ain't out of ours," Hugh said. "And, unless I miss my guess, bounty hunters are gonna be thicker than fleas on a dog's back before long."

"You saying that reward money will draw them this far off the beaten path?"

"What do you think?"

"Sure hope you're wrong. T. J. Littlejohn was the only bounty hunter I ever met that was worth a pinch of snuff."

The sheriff thumbed his hat brim to Miss Sadie, turned and walked out the door.

# Chapter X

Mary was tucking Sally into bed. She leaned over and placed a soft kiss on her daughter's forehead.

"Momma, when is bubby coming home?"

The young girl's simple question shattered Mary's heart. She caught her breath and tried to swallow the huge lump that swelled her throat. With a quavering voice she whispered the only answer she could give.

"Soon, Tad will be home soon."

It had been more than two weeks since Tad and Lupe rode away. Almost nightly, after the girls were asleep, Mary stood on the front porch, sometimes for hours, staring up at the stars, praying, and wondering if somewhere, her son might be looking at those same twinkling specks of light.

*Please, Lord, keep my son safe. I lost my husband and I couldn't bear to lose my son, too.*

A soft wind caressed her face. Somewhere a whip-o-will called to its mate. The black velvet night wrapped around her, gathering her into its presence.

Memories crept out of the dark. Visions of T. J. flooded Mary's senses. She closed her eyes to shut out the hurt, but his memory dwelled in her mind and in her heart and would not be denied.

She saw him as she had seen him that very first time, riding tall and proud past her father's church house. She saw those dark, penetrating eyes as they locked on her, penetrating past her own, right into her very soul.

She had no earthly idea who he was or where he came from, she only knew in that instant this was the man God sent to her. He was the man she wanted to spend the rest of her life with.

Her father had objected. 'He's nothing but a drifting half-breed. He'll never amount to nothing', he had told her. But Mary felt her father was more concerned with what his congregation would think about the reverend's daughter marrying a half-breed Indian than anything.

In the end, when it became clear to him that she was going to marry T. J., he turned her out of the house. She had never seen either of her parents alive again.

Mary and T. J. dreamed of building a home here in this valley. Together, they worked side-by-side to make the dream a reality. They built a home, and a family, and a happy life. A life that Mary had assumed would last to watch their children and grandchildren grow up.

But destiny had betrayed her.

She opened her eyes and blinked the night into focus around her. Her thoughts scattered and she felt the ever -present emptiness, the familiar raw aches of loss, confusion, and loneliness gnaw at her insides. She took a shuddery breath and swiped at the tears with the back of a hand.

Out of the darkness of her mind another image took shape. George Paxton. Thoughts of him seemed to be more frequent in recent days. He was a good man, probably as lonely as she was. Neither was there doubt that he loved her. She saw it in his eyes even before her husband's death because a woman's intuition tells her those things; but, more and more lately, it became apparent how much he cared for her. She cared for him, too, and enjoyed his company, but did she love him? Could she ever love another man the way she loved T. J.?

Her mind returned painfully to the scene in the dusty street of Lubbock after he was shot and to T. J.'s final words to George. "Watch after my family," he had told his friend.

Mary had heard her husband's whispered words and seen George's quick glance at her and the surprised look on his face.

Was T. J.'s request simply for his friend to watch out for their safety? Or did his final request hold more meaning?

George Paxton sat at his desk, shuffling papers, but his mind was not on his work. His every thought lately was of Mary Littlejohn. Images of her flashed through his mind. He thought of her long, golden hair that hung well below her tiny waist, her flashing, sky-blue eyes that laughed when she did. The way her beautiful lips curled up at one corner when she smiled. The way she carried herself as she moved about the kitchen, smooth, graceful as a mountain lioness. *Lord, she's a beautiful woman.*

His thoughts were scattered when the door to his office was opened suddenly and Silas Isaacs hobbled in.

"Thought you'd be wanting to know, George, two strangers just rode into town. Judging by their looks and the tied down pistols they be wearing, they ain't cow punchers looking fer work. They were askin' about Hugh Overstreet."

"Is that so? What'd you tell em?"

"Didn't tell them nothing. Didn't figure it was any of their business."

"Where are they now?"

"They bedded down their horses and headed fer the saloon."

"I'm obliged, Silas," George said, rising from his chair and clamping his hat on his head. "I'll see what they want."

"Want me to tag along?"

"Naw, I'll handle it."

Silas followed him out the door, and then turned toward the livery. George headed along the boardwalk toward the saloon up the street.

The Ace High saloon was unusually busy. The sun was still an hour high, yet a dozen horses stood along the hitch rail. George gentled his Colt in his holster and pushed through the door.

A quick sweeping glance revealed four local-types playing cards at a table. Another five punchers from one of the nearby ranches were nursing beer at a table. It was the two strangers lounging at the bar that captured George's attention.

One was a tall, slim fellow, wide in the shoulders and small-waisted. He had long, black, shoulder length hair. A tied down, pearl-handled Colt hung in a cut-away holster on his left leg, the sure sign of a gunfighter.

His companion was a burly fellow that hadn't missed many meals. He too, wore a tied-down pistol. George had seen their kind before. They were trouble with a capital T.

George headed their way.

"Afternoon, Sheriff," Sam greeted from behind the bar.

"Afternoon, Sam. Give me a beer."

The bartender drew a mug full of the golden-colored liquid and set it in front of the lawman.

George glanced up at the long mirror behind the bar as he took a long swig. Both of the strangers were staring back at him in the mirror.

"You boys just riding through?"

"You could say that," the tall one replied.

"You got a name?"

"Cy Turley. This is my brother, he goes by Shorty."

"Where you call home?"

"Any place I decide to hang my hat. Any law against that?"

"Might be, might not. We got a peaceful little town here. They pay me to keep it that way."

"That ain't exactly a hospitable welcome, Sheriff."

"Hospitality depends on the conduct of the guest. You boys are guests in our town. Get my meaning?"

"Ain't never left a place until I was ready to go. Don't aim to start now."

"Then keep that Colt where it belongs."

George drained the mug of beer in a single gulp and flipped a coin to the bar tender.

"Be seeing you, Sam."

"So long, Sheriff."

Back in his office, George thumbed through a stack of wanted posters. The name, Turley, rang a bell. He knew he'd heard that name before, he just couldn't remember where. Finding no fliers by that name he poured himself a cup of leftover coffee and settled back in his chair to think.

Then it hit him. *Of course, Turley, that was the name of the three brothers Hugh Overstreet gunned down in Abilene a year or so ago. No wonder they were asking Silas about Hugh. They're kin folk, maybe even brothers likely here to settle a score with Hugh. Good thing he's gone. Maybe when they learn he's not here they'll ride on. Hope so anyway.*

Something was gnawing at him inside his stomach, and that usually meant trouble. He decided he best take a turn around town just to make sure. He retrieved his hat from the peg beside the door and stepped out into the cold, clear night wind.

He stood for a long minute scanning both ways up and down the dark street. Rosco, the black piano player in the Ace High saloon was playing one of his lonesome tunes. George listened for a while, staring up into the dark sky.

It was a clear night. A million stars winked from a cloudless sky. The thin slice of a sickle moon offered little light.

Suddenly a shot rang out, then another. They came from the direction of the saloon. Before the echo died away George was headed that way in a long-legged trot.

He paused just outside the door and slipped his Colt from its holster and thumbed back the hammer. A sweeping glance revealed a cowboy lying in a gathering pool of blood. His four companions were sitting motionless at the table with their hands pressed palm down.

The two Turley brothers stood with their backs to the bar. Both held a pistol in one hand and a drink in the other. Sam, the bartender, stood behind the bar with a frightened look on his face. George raised his pistol and stepped inside.

"Drop the guns, boys!" George said loudly. "I'll only say it once."

He focused his stare on the noses of the Turley's pistols for any movement in his direction. Several long heartbeats passed before the men dropped their weapons to the floor.

"It was self defense," the one called Shorty said. "That cow nurse went for his gun first. He was too slow."

George walked over and picked up the pistols. He lifted them to his nose. Both had been fired.

"Turn around and put your hands on the bar, both of you."

"What for," Shorty protested. "We ain't done nothing but protect ourselves."

"We'll see, now do what I said."

The two men slowly turned and placed both of their hands flat on the bar. George patted them down for hide-away weapons. He found none.

"What happened here, Sam?" the Sheriff asked.

"These fellows and those boys over there got to jawing at one another. Things got out of hand. One thing led to another. The one called Tobey lost his head and drew, or at least he started to. Both of these fellows shot him before his pistol cleared leather."

"See there!" Shorty said sarcastically. "I told you it was self defense."

George wheeled to face the speaker. "Shut your mouth! I know those boys. I don't know you two. Besides, I warned both of you not to cause any trouble in my town. Seems you don't hear none too good. Let's go."

For the first time the slim one spoke up.

"Go where?"

"To jail."

"What's the charge?"

"Pick one, disturbing the peace, for now, I'll think of something else on the way, now let's go."

"You ain't taking me to..."

The big one's words were cut off in mid-sentence as George swung his pistol barrel in a backward arc that struck the man along his left ear, dropping him to the floor like a sack of potatoes.

George swung a look and his Colt to fix on the slim gunfighter. He saw only cold hatred festering in the man's eyes.

"You got anything to say?" He asked the gunfighter.

"Not for now. But this ain't the end of it."

"Then maybe I better put an end to it and just shoot you where you stand."

The gunman's eyes went wide. It was clear he didn't know

whether to believe the lawman or not. He flicked a glance at his brother on the floor at his feet, then back to George. Tiny beads of sweat popped out on his forehead.

"Pick up your brother and move before I change my mind. You're both going to jail."

"I can't lift him."

"Then drag him by his boots. Now move!"

# Chapter XI

Over coffee, Hugh, Tad, and Lupe discussed their strategy as to how they were going to accomplish their mission.

"My suggestion is that I ride out to the Slade ranch pretending that I'm looking for a job. That way I can get the feel of the place and see how things stack up. Maybe you boys can nose around town, find out everything you can. We need to know when Slade comes to town and if he brings anybody with him and, if so, how many. How does that sound? Anybody got any better ideas?"

"Sounds good to me, Tad said.

"We can start with Señor Hernandez, my friend at the livery," Lupe told them.

"Good."

"Didn't mean to listen in," Sadie said, walking up with a fresh pot of coffee. "Some of that bunch from Slade's Two-Bar S ranch is in here most every day. Don't know how they ever get any work done."

"Does Slade himself ever come to town?"

"Very seldom, that I know anything about. Higgins, over at the general store, or the new bar keeper over at the saloon might know more about it than I do."

"Much obliged, Sadie."

The three finished their coffee, paid for their meal, and headed for the livery.

The old livery man was pitching hay into the corral that held three slat ribbed horses that looked like they had been rode hard and put away wet.

"You fellows are up and about mighty early."

"Morning, old timer," Hugh greeted. "Them critters look like they've seen better days."

"Ain't we all?" the old hostler cackled, spitting a stream of brown tobacco juice that stained the sandy soil.

"Reckon you're right there."

*"Buenos dias, señor."* Lupe greeted.

*"Buenos dias,* Lupe."

"What you fellows up to this morning?" The hostler inquired.

"Tell us what you know about Buck Slade's place," Tad asked.

"What you looking to know?"

"Anything and everything you can think of," Hugh told him, leaning against the split-corral fence and chewing on a piece of straw. "How do I find it? How many riders does he employ?"

"To hear him tell it, you're standing on it. He thinks he owns the whole country and wants it all. He's forced several outfits into selling their spreads to him at his price. Those that refuse, end up either burned out or shot up. His neighbors are sick and tired of it. They've all got together. They're hiring gun hands just like Slade is doing. There's gonna be an all out range war sure as shootin'.

"Slade's headquarters is a few hours ride northwest toward the San Andres Mountains. You don't have to worry none about finding the ranch, his men will find you. He's got patrols thick as fleas on a dog's back

"I've been out there a time or two to shoe horses or deliver a buckboard. There's the usual barns and stock corrals and bunk houses, but the Hacienda is something to behold. It's built like a fort and guarded better. If'n I was you, I wouldn't bother riding all that way without an invite. I hear tell they shoot first and ask a man's business later."

"Sounds like a right friendly bunch," Hugh said.

"Well, there's friendly and there's friendly. Buck Slade don't qualify in either batch."

"Got any notion how many riders Slade's got?"

"Way too many for the size of his herd. Oh, he's got some punchers, sure enough, but most of his men look more like gun hands than cow nurses."

"Hmm, interesting."

"You still thinking about riding out there, Mr. Overstreet?" Tad asked.

"Yeah, I want to have a look-see with my own eyes. I might not be back for a day or two, you boys make yourselves at home until you hear from me."

Within minutes Hugh had saddled his horse and rode out. Tad and Lupe sat down on a bale of hay and continued their visit with the old hostler.

Riding north out of town, as the liveryman had instructed, Hugh skirted a huge oak tree that crowded the road on the edge of town. Its sprawling branches reached far out over the road. Turning northwest, the barren prairie seemed to stretch endlessly.

He wondered why anyone would build a ranch in this barren land, let alone a town. Clusters of scrubby creosote bushes crowded the faint road. Staghorn cholla reached long arms toward the cloudless sky.

In the distance, a line of mountains the old hostler had called the San Andres rose against a backdrop of limitless sky and marched northward like an unbroken column of sentinels.

The closer he got to the mountains, the greener the countryside became. A small stream meandered across the landscape, bringing its life-giving nourishment to the dry and thirsty land.

Clumps of lush grama grass became more abundant and he began to understand why a rancher would locate in this area.

To his right, the form of a distant rider took shape, then another on his left. Both paralleled his course. As the outriders closed the distance between them, Hugh thumbed the traveling loop from the hammer of his Colt and continued toward his destination.

As the riders grew closer, two more appeared in front of him, riding to intercept him. *Looks like the old hostler was right,* he thought, *seems they ain't big on company.* He drew rein and waited.

The four riders galloped up to him in a cloud of dust. Each had a Winchester in his hands. They reined up, blocking his way with their rifles propped on their legs. These were no cowboys. These were hardened gun hands if he ever saw them.

The obvious leader rode a gray gelding. He had a square jaw and a dangerous look in his pale gray eyes. He wore a belly holster that held an ivory handled Colt.

"You're on Two Bar S range, mister."

"I heard Buck Slade might be hiring."

"We got plenty of punchers."

"I ain't looking to wet nurse cows, that ain't my line of work."

"And just what might be your *line of work*?"

"I convince people to do what they don't want to do. Now if we're through with the niceties, I come to see the boss."

"The boss don't see nobody he didn't invite, and you ain't invited."

"You got a name?"

"Yeah, I got a name. Folks call me Clay Asher, you might have heard of me."

"I heard of you. I heard you were a back shooter from Texas."

"You got a big mouth, mister. I didn't catch your name."

"I didn't offer it. And you've got about two heartbeats to wheel that horse around and take me to Slade before I blow you out of your saddle."

Disbelief and surprise widened the leader's eyes. The muzzle of his rifle began its downward journey to level.

Faster than the eye could follow, Hugh drew his Colt and fired. The pistol belched fire and hot lead. A black hole appeared in the man's left shirt pocked. Crimson blood spurted forth even as he tumbled backwards from the saddle. In the same fluid motion Hugh's smoking pistol swung to cover the remaining three shocked riders.

"I asked to see the boss. I don't ask twice."

After disarming the men and having them tie their newly departed companion across his saddle, Hugh rode behind them as they led him to the ranch headquarters.

They rode toward the mountains. The countryside got greener. Runoff from the mountains created a network of small streams, nourished the soil and produced lush, green grass that covered the ground thick and fetlock high.

Ahead, nestled among the rolling foothills, a magnificent Hacienda stood like a castle perched on a sloping hillside. High walls completely surrounded the large, enclosed area. A well-traveled road led to two heavy-looking double gates that allowed entrance. Again, the old hostler's description, that it looked more like a fort than a home, was right on the money.

Numerous barns, bunkhouses, outbuildings and corrals were situated in a community-like jumble a quarter mile away. Two dozen or so hands were gathered around a corral watching a cowboy break a mustang. Shouts of encouragement and cowboy yells gave the place a festive atmosphere,

A bell sounded as they approached the opening in the wall of the compound surrounding the Hacienda. Several riders from around the corral mounted horses and galloped to meet them.

Hugh and his *escorts* walked their mounts through the wide gates and reined up at a wrought iron hitching rail just inside the gate. A welcoming committee delegation was approaching from the direction of the main house along a flower-edged cobblestone path.

Hugh swung a leg across the saddle and settled it on the ground. The three riders sat their saddles. One held the reins to the horse carrying the body of Clay Asher.

Although Hugh had never laid eyes on Buck Slade, there was little doubt the man leading the group approaching them with long-legged strides was the back-shooting killer that Tad had sworn to bring in dead or alive.

Behind him, a couple of paces walked a young fellow that was a younger version of the big rancher and was obviously his son. Another cocky young man with a messed up face had to be the one that T. J. had cold-cocked with the barrel of his shotgun. He looked a mess. Most of his front teeth were gone. His top lip sagged at one corner and a deep, purplish scar ran across his cheek.

Buck Slade was impressive, no doubt about it. He was tall, most likely standing well over six feet. He was corded and lean, all rawboned muscle. His wide shoulders and narrow waist were evident even beneath the short, Mexican jacket he wore. Salt and pepper hair pushed out from under the black, flat crowned hat that was ringed by a hat band with silver conchos. He had a square jaw and faded blue eyes that right now, stared hard at Hugh. A cruel twist to his lips gave him an angry look. Cinched about his waist was a black holster holding a pearl-handled, nickel-plated Colt.

"What's all this?" The big man demanded. "Who is this fellow? Who is that across the saddle?"

"That's Clay," one of the riders answered meekly. "This fellow gunned him down slicker'n a whistle. He's faster'n scat. Then he took our guns away from us."

"One man faced all four of you down and shot Clay? Get out of my sight and take that body with you."

Buck Slade's angry attention swung in Hugh's direction and pinned him with a hard, searching stare.

"Who are you?" he demanded.

"Name's Overstreet, Hugh Overstreet from Texas."

"Am I supposed to know the name?"

"I know the name," a voice from one of the riders that just arrived said quietly, barely above a whisper.

It was Hugh's turn to swing a look. The speaker was a tall, skeleton-skinny fellow dressed completely in black. His tanned, leathery-looking skin was stretched thin and tight over high cheek bones, giving the appearance that he would be more at home in a coffin instead of riding the big, black gelding. Two, cross-draw pistols rode easy-looking at his waist.

*Ace Bonham,* Hugh thought. *The Texas gunfighter said to have killed over twenty men.*

Their eyes met and held for a long moment. Bonham had glassy-looking gray eyes. They bored into Hugh and took his measure, one inch at a time.

"Ace," Hugh said.

"So you're the famous Hugh Overstreet? I had you figured

to be ten foot tall and breathing fire out your nose, from all the stories that's going around."

"That's only when I get riled."

"So you took Clay, huh? He was pretty quick."

"Must have got lucky, I guess."

"Uh-huh, I reckon. Mr. Slade, this fellow is known far and wide in Texas. Some say he's the fastest gun around, though I'd argue the point."

"What brings you to Two Bar S, Mr. Overstreet?" Buck Slade asked, fixing a gaze on Hugh.

"It's like I tried to tell your hired help, I heard you might be hiring. Especially now that it seems you're one man short."

Something resembling a faint smile lifted one corner of the rancher's lips.

"Seems I am, now that you mention it. Come on in the house and let's talk over a brandy."

"Don't drink, but coffee would go good."

"I think coffee can be arranged. These are my sons, Brad, my oldest, and Billy.

Hugh nodded and followed the rancher and his two sons into the house.

"We don't get many visitors out here," the rancher said over his shoulder as they were walking.

"I can see why," Hugh told him.

Hugh took in the place with a sweeping gaze. The Hacienda was beautiful. Hugh had been in lots of places and seen lots of things, but he had never seen anything like this. It was a low-roofed adobe structure. Large lodge pole support beams protruded through the thick walls. Red clay tile covered the entire structure. A wide, covered veranda seemed to wrap completely around the large building. Colorful hanging baskets of flowers lined the edge of the porch.

Slade pushed open a heavy, hand carved door. Hugh stepped in, the two sons followed. They entered into an inner courtyard laced with cobblestone walkways, a well- tended flower garden, and featuring a spring fed fountain and fish pond, complete with water lilies and gold fish.

Surrounding the square courtyard were numerous doors, obviously leading to separate rooms in the huge Hacienda.

*This is the way to live*, Hugh thought. Instead he said, "Nice place."

"Thanks."

Walking along the pathway, they passed several doors. Slade stopped, opened, and ushered his guest into an elaborately decorated den. The rock fireplace extended from floor to ceiling. Two black, overstuffed leather chairs were situated in front of the roaring fire. A small table sat between them.

"Please be seated, Mr. Overstreet."

Hugh sank into the soft, comfortable chair. The two sons folded onto a nearby couch that matched the chairs. Two young, Mexican house girls hurried in with silver trays, one held a bottle of brandy and several glasses, the other a silver pot of steaming coffee.

"You live pretty good," Hugh said.

"When I came here there was nothing. I built this ranch from scratch. I fought Indians, Comanchero, bandits, and land squatters. Over the years my ranch has grown until it now encompasses over a hundred thousand acres and it's still growing."

"So I hear."

"Exactly *what* did you hear?

"I heard talk that some of your neighbors sold out mighty cheap after some, not so friendly, persuasion. I also heard they have banded together and formed a cattlemen's association to stop your expansion. If that's true, you're gonna need all the help you can get."

"They have nothing to say about my expansion.  I'll do

whatever I please and I'll crush anyone that gets in my way. So, you'd like to work for me?"

"That depends. I don't come cheap and I don't nurse cows."

"And exactly what do you do then?"

"I do what I do, same as half the crew you got working for you, only better."

"I see. As you said earlier, it seems we do have an opening. We might be able to use you. The job pays a hundred a month. That's almost three times the going rate for a ranch hand."

"I ain't no ranch hand. I lose that much in a poker game on Saturday night."

"And just what would you expect for your *services*?"

"Two hundred a month plus a thousand dollar bonus for *special jobs*."

"I'm afraid that's out of the question."

Hugh drained the last swallow of coffee, pushed up from the chair, and clamped his hat on his head.

"Then I reckon we don't have nothing more to talk about. I'm obliged for the coffee."

"If you should reconsider my offer, just let me know."

"Don't hold that job open on my account, Mr. Slade. Good day."

The sun was playing hide-and-seek with the western horizon as Hugh rode back into Alamogordo. He reined up at the livery. The old hostler limped up and took the reins as Hugh swung stiffly to the ground.

"You find Slade's place?"

"I found it, right where you said it would be."

"Mr. McKenzie stopped by awhile ago looking for you. Said he'd like to talk. Said he'd be down at the saloon for awhile."

"Who's this McKenzie, fellow?"

"He's got a ranch south of Slade's place. He's the head of the ranchers association."

"What does he look like?"

"Tall fellow, wide shoulders, gray hair, looks like a cattle man."

"Where's Tad and Lupe?"

"They hung around here most of the day. That Lupe shore has growed up. He wears that pistol like he was born with it tied to his leg. Most likely you'll find them down at Sadie's place."

"Much obliged, old timer."

Hugh pushed through the door to the saloon. He allowed a sweeping glance to travel around the room, finally settling on the big rancher. He was sitting at a table against the back wall listening to a hard-case type that was doing most of the talking.

Hugh bellied up to the bar and asked the bar tender for a beer. As he sipped the lukewarm liquid he watched McKenzie and the hard case out of the corner of his eye.

"Sorry, Mr. Van Horn," Hugh heard McKenzie say, "but like I said, we can't use you."

"Well, if that ain't a howdy-do." the hard case shouted, jumping up and kicking away the chair. "I rode all the way up here from Hobbs cause I heard tell you was hiring. Ain't I good enough for you?"

Hugh watched the big rancher closely. He wanted to see how he handled himself.

"Good enough ain't got nothing to do with it. I said I can't use you. That's the end of it."

"Not by a long shot," the man shouted, his hand only a hair's breath from the butt of his pistol. "Stand up!"

"I ain't wearing a gun," the rancher said evenly, without a trace of fear.

It was clear to Hugh that the hard case wasn't about to drop it. He had a mad on and somebody was gonna get hurt.

"I am," Hugh spoke up.

The one called Van Horn twisted a look over his shoulder at Hugh.

"This ain't none of your affair."

"The man said he wasn't wearing a pistol. You best drop it."

The man squared around facing Hugh. He was itching for a fight. He spread his feet and dropped into a gunfighter's crouch, his hand hovering just above the shiny pistol on his right leg. He flexed his long fingers.

"Maybe you don't know who I am, mister. My name's Van Horn. You might have heard of me."

"Can't say I have. But you got two ways to go here, Mr. Van Horn. The easy one is to turn and walk out, climb on your horse and put as many tracks between me and you as you can. The other way is to twitch your hand any closer to that pistol, and I just might have to kill you."

"That's mighty big talk. You got a name?"

"Overstreet, Hugh Overstreet."

The man's eyes rimmed white and his jaw dropped. He licked his suddenly dry lips. His hands raised slowly, carefully, head high, and away from his gun, palms open.

"You're...I had no idea. I didn't mean no harm, Mr. Overstreet."

"Could've fooled me. Ain't there someplace else you need to be?"

"Yeah, I mean, I was just leaving."

Van Horn headed for the door, gaining speed with every step. By the time he reached the bat wings, he was in a full trot. Every eye in the room watched him go. Several chuckles broke the thick silence.

"I'd like to buy you a beer, Mr. Overstreet," McKenzie said.

"Thanks, but one is my limit." Hugh said, walking over to the rancher's table. "I heard you wanted to talk?"

"Indeed, please, sit down. I have a proposition for you."

"Oh?"

"I understand you rode out to the Slade ranch today?"

"I did."

"Am I to assume that you are now in his employ?"

"If you did, you'd be wrong."

"Glad to hear it. I'm Alan McKenzie," the rancher said, sticking out a work-hardened hand. "I've got a little place north of here, not much, few hundred acres, run a couple hundred head."

Hugh took it. The rancher's handshake was firm. "You already know my name."

"Your reputation precedes you, Mr. Overstreet."

"So it seems. What you got on your mind, Mr. McKenzie?"

"We'd like to hire you."

"Who's *we*?"

"I'm president of the Cattleman's Association. I'm sure you've already heard about the trouble between the local ranchers and Slade? He's set his mind on running all of us out of business and taking over our spreads. We ain't about to let that happen."

"How you plan on stopping him? He's got fifty or more riders, all hardened gun hands. You and your Association ready for a range war?"

"If that's what it takes."

"All due respect, Mr. McKenzie, but I doubt you know what you're getting into. A range war is like a prairie fire, it destroys everything and everyone in its path. The only survivors are the ones that get out of its way."

"Then what are you saying we ought to do, just tuck tail and run, and let him take what he wants without a fight?"

"Ain't saying that at all, I'm saying a snake is harmless without its head. Cut off the head and you solve the problem."

"And how do we do that?"

"I got a notion that problem will take care of itself."

Hugh reached into his pocket and withdrew the 'dead or alive' wanted poster on Buck Slade. He slowly unfolded it and pushed it across the table to the rancher.

"You ever see this?"

McKenzie stared at the flier for a long minute, a hint of a thin smile lifting the right side of his moustache.

"Well, I'll be a monkey's uncle. I had no idea Slade was a wanted man."

"Before long this place will be crawling with bounty hunters looking to put some jingle in their pockets."

"Is that why you're here?"

"Nope, but I'm siding a couple of boys that I think mighty high of. One of them is T. J. Littlejohn's boy. Slade murdered his pa, shot him in the back. He's got it in mind to settle the score."

"I remember Littlejohn. He's the fellow that messed up Billy Slade's face with the barrel of a shotgun and clipped Buck's tail feathers ain't he?"

"That's the one. Slade never forgot it and followed him all the way to Texas and bushwhacked him."

"So you're suggesting we just bide our time for awhile?"

"That's what I would do if I was you."

"This has been a mighty informative chat, Mr. Overstreet, I'm obliged."

# Chapter XII

Hugh, Tad, and Lupe were on their way to dinner at Sadie's. They stepped out of the hotel door onto the boardwalk just as a lone rider rode slowly down the dusty street of Alamogordo.

Something about him caught Hugh's attention. The rider sat slouched in the saddle of a big chestnut gelding. His long, black duster hung to the top of his boots and flapped in a westerly wind. His flat-brimmed hat was sweat-stained around the crown and pulled low, partially hiding his leathery face from the sun. A Sharps .52 caliber buffalo gun rode in a saddle boot under his right stirrup leather.

He was a big man. Big and tall and thin as a fence post. His dark, flashing eyes flicked from one side to the other, a sure sign of a man familiar with trouble.

When the rider came abreast with Hugh and the boys, he gentled back on the geldings reins and sat his saddle. His dark eyes settled squarely on Hugh Overstreet and lingered for a long heartbeat.

"Hugh," he said, the raspy voice sounding like fingernails on a sheet-iron roof.

"Clint," Hugh acknowledged. "It's been awhile."

"That it has."

The mysterious rider touched finger and thumb to his hat brim and heeled his mount on down the street.

"Who was that, Mr. Overstreet?" Lupe asked, as he watched the rider rein up at the hitching rail in front of the saloon.

"Boys, that was the one and only Clint Sinclair. He's a working bounty hunter from up in Wyoming, one of the best in the business. Times must be tough, can't think of any other reason he would be this far off his range for a five hundred dollar reward."

"Maybe he's here to go to work for Slade, or the Cattleman's Association." Tad said.

"Nope, not Sinclair, he's a killer, sure enough, but he's his own man. He's here for that bounty, no doubt about it."

"You think there will be others?" Tad asked.

"Just as sure as God made little green apples. You boys go on down to Sadie's, I'll be along."

Tad and Lupe headed up the street to the restaurant. Hugh angled across the street toward the saloon.

Hugh found Sinclair sitting at a table near the back of the room with his back to the wall. He was sipping a beer with his left hand. His eyes flicked to every movement, every sound and his right hand rested comfortably only inches from the black handled pistol in a belly holster.

"Off your range a bit, ain't you?" Hugh said, sliding out a chair and folding into it.

"Pickings are mighty slim up Wyoming way. Occurs to me you're a long ways from Texas, too."

"Well, I was kinda in the neighborhood."

"Hate you rode all that way for nothing. You after this, Slade fellow too?"

"Man has to make a living. Times are hard down in Texas."

Hugh settled a gaze on the man before him. Sinclair had pale blue eyes, sunk back into a leathery face that told a story of miles of lonely trails and sleepless nights. When the eyes squinted they went more than a little hard.

"I wouldn't start counting my money, was I you, I'm aiming to collect the bounty on this jasper. Got any idea where he hangs out?"

"Ain't no secret, just head northwest and keep riding until somebody objects. Best watch your backside though."

"So it's that kind of set up, huh? Kinda figured as much, you being so helpful and all."

"What are friends for?"

"Friends? The way I hear it, you ain't got a friend to your name."

"Slade's got some fellows riding for him you might know."

"They got a name?"

"Ace Bonham, for one."

"Bonham, huh? Never did like that back shooter. Crooked as a barrel full of snakes. He got a flier on him these days?"

"Wouldn't be surprised."

"Anybody else?"

"Mostly small-time. One named, Clay Asher, I had to shoot him. I saw Tomlin, from the Indian Territory, and that kid from Missouri, can't think of his name."

"Damon Plummer?"

"That's the one."

"This Slade fellow is serious about staying alive, ain't he?"

"Ain't just that, there's a range war brewing. Slade's gobbling up all the land. He's hiring gun slicks to hurry the hold-outs to sell out to him, at his price, of course. He's got fifty or more already. There's a bunch of folks that are taking exception. They've formed a Cattleman's Association."

"I ain't interested in getting involved in a range war. Might be a little harder than I thought to collect that five hundred, but it will happen. I'll just collect my money and ride on."

Hugh couldn't help noticing the lines of concern that wrinkled the corners of the bounty hunter's eyes as four men stomped in the front door of the saloon. One of them was the gun slick from Missouri, the one they had just talked about.

"Say you shot Asher?" Sinclair asked, his gaze never leaving the four newcomers. "I heard he was pretty swift."

"A man can hear all sorts of things."

"Uh-huh, ain't it the truth? He worth any bounty?"

"Like as not."

The four newcomers had bellied up to the bar and ordered drinks. One of them turned his back to the bar and leaned his elbows on it, his gaze swept the room and settled on Sinclair and Overstreet. He leaned over and whispered something to the man standing next to him, kid from Missouri.

*Damon Plummer ain't old enough to grow whiskers,* Hugh thought, but the Colt tied low on his left leg belied his boyish face.

"Hey, you! Old man!" the kid said loudly. "You the one that gunned down Clay Asher?"

A thin grin wrinkled the corner of Sinclair's mouth.

"I believe the kid must be talking to you since you're the only *old man* in the whole place."

"You talking to me, *sonny*." Hugh said, twisting a look over his shoulder.

"Yeah, *Old Man,* I'm talking to *you.* Somebody said you're claiming to be Hugh Overstreet, the gun fighter. I say you're lying. I don't think you're him."

"Don't matter if I'm him or I ain't. What matters is that you just called me a liar. I'm gonna count to three before I stand up. If I ain't heard you apologize before then, I'm gonna kill you, *sonny.*"

"I'm Damon Plummer. Nobody talks to me like that!"

"One."

"Well, *are you* Overstreet or not?"

"Two."

"You're bluffing, mister. I'm calling your bluff."

The young gun slick's friends backed out of the line of fire. From his sitting position, Hugh fixed his over the shoulder stare, on the young gun fighter's eyes. He waited. They blinked. By the time the man had finished blinking, Hugh stood, drew, thumbed back the hammer of his Smith & Wesson .44, raised it to eye level, and aimed it squarely at the startled man's chest.

"Three."

The young gun slick's hand hadn't even reached his pistol. A sudden panic attack distorted his face. Great drops of sweat popped out on his forehead. His widened eyes flicked from side to side, as if searching for someone, anyone, to help him.

Still holding his cocked pistol at arm's length, Hugh closed the distance between them until the nose of his pistol was jammed inches deep into the boy's open mouth.

"Listen to me, *sonny boy,* cause I ain't gonna say this but once. The next time I lay eyes on you I'm gonna kill you, understand? There won't be no counting, no nothing. You're in the wrong profession, *sonny.* You best get on your horse and ride fast and far. Nod your head if you're getting my meaning."

The youngster stood shaking, wall-eyed with fright written all over his face, apparently knowing that he was only a finger pull from death. He nodded emphatically.

"That goes for the rest of you boys too. Anybody want to argue the point?"

The young man's companions shook their heads and headed for the door. As Hugh headed back to Clint Sinclair's table, the sound of galloping hooves could be heard clearly, headed south.

"See you haven't lost your touch, *Old son,*" Sinclair laughed, raising his glass to Hugh in a toast.

\* \* \*

The pre-dawn grayness tinged the eastern sky as Buck Slade strolled casually from his sprawling hacienda with a steaming cup of coffee in his hand. He loved the freshness of early mornings. The wind was out of the north, and cottony clouds scudded across a lightening sky.

He was pleased with himself. His dream of building a ranching empire was rapidly becoming reality. Before long he would own more land than most men could even imagine. He would be able to ride for days in any direction and never leave land that belonged to him. Land meant power. Buck Slade meant to be the most powerful man in the New Mexico Territory.

There was talk of New Mexico becoming a state. When that happened he meant to be its first governor. Governor, Buck Slade, he liked the way that sounded.

His musings were interrupted by the hurried approach of Ace Bonham, his foreman.

"Mr. Slade, I thought you'd want to know, four of the boys didn't come back from town last night."

"Why should that concern me? Maybe they got drunk and are sleeping it off before making the ride back."

"I thought about that, but I don't think so, two of them was supposed to relieve the line riders today. They know the penalty for not being where they're supposed to be when they're supposed to be there. They know it would cost them their jobs. That new hot shot kid from Missouri is one of them."

"You mean the Plummer kid? I'd hate to lose him."

"Yeah, that's him."

"What do you think has happened to them?"

"Don't know, but I intend to find out. I'm riding into town and see what's going on."

"Very well, let me know as soon as you get back."

* * *

The sun cast long, mid-morning shadows across the dusty street of Alamogordo. Ace Bonham rode slowly down the street and reined up in front of the saloon. He figured that would be the place to start in discovering what happened to four of his men.

Since it was still mid-morning the hitching rail was empty. He looped the reins and did a quick half-hitch. Stepping up onto the boardwalk, he paused to roll a cigarette, wet the edge with his tongue, and lit it with a match raked across his leather chaps. He took a long, satisfying drag and swept the street with a searching gaze, thinking maybe he could spot the horses of his missing men. But saw nothing of them.

For a small, one-horse town, Alamogordo was a busy place. Heavy freight wagons lumbered past, piled high and pulled by a two hitch team of heavy work horses.

Women in work dresses, covered by bib aprons and wearing colorful bonnets hurried down the street carrying straw baskets full of groceries.

From across the street, a man stepped out of the hotel, paused on the boardwalk to gaze up and down the street. *Something about that fellow looks familiar,* Ace thought, studying the man and searching his memory.

When their eyes met he remembered. *Clint Sinclair.* The deadly Wyoming bounty hunter. *Wonder what he is doing here in New Mexico Territory?*

Ace had run into Sinclair a time or two in one town or another. He had never liked or trusted the bounty hunter. Something about the man that worried Ace, like Sinclair was always on the prod, always looking for an excuse to tangle with him.

He had never actually seen Sinclair use a gun, but he had

heard talk. Those that had seen the bounty hunter in action said that he was greased lightning with a pistol.

Not anxious for trouble, Ace turned on his heel and walked into the saloon. It was empty. Not a soul other than the fat, bald-headed bar tender with a dirty-white apron and a mutton-chop moustache.

"Morning, Mr. Bonham. You're out and around mighty early, what'll you have this morning?"

"Give me a double shot of rye and some information."

"Information is free. Rye will be two-bits."

"Four of my men rode into town yesterday. They were supposed to be back last night. They never showed up. Seen anything of them?"

"Yeah, they were in here. One of them, the kid, roostered up to Hugh Overstreet like he had a cocklebur under his saddle about something. He was on the prod, no two ways about it."

"What happened?"

"Overstreet is one tough old man. He handled the kid like it was child's play. Never seen anything like it."

"You gonna tell me what happened or you gonna flap your jaw all day?"

"The kid called Overstreet a liar. That was his first mistake. Overstreet told him if he didn't apologize by the time he counted to three, that he was gonna kill him, all the time he was sitting over yonder at that table with his back to the kid."

The bar tender paused and started wiping glasses with a white bar towel.

"Well, what happened?"

"Overstreet started counting, still sitting there calm as all get out. The kid was braced and ready. When Overstreet reached the count of three, not sure what happened. It was too fast to see.

"One minute he was sitting there in the chair with his back

to the kid, the next thing anybody knew Overstreet was standing with his pistol out and cocked. The kid never had a chance. His hand never got halfway to his gun."

"You saying Overstreet shot the kid in cold blood?"

"Ain't what I'm saying at all. Overstreet walked right up to the kid and stuck the barrel of his Colt in the kid's mouth. He told the kid to hightail it out of town and that the next time he saw him he would shoot him on sight. He said the same went for your other men too. The last I heard was those fellows riding hell bent for leather south out of town."

Ace's face was crimson red with anger. He threw back his head and swallowed the double rye in a single gulp and slammed the shot glass down hard on the bar.

"Give me another! That old man has caused me way too much trouble already. About time somebody took him down a notch or two."

"I'd be mighty careful about talk like that was I you," a raspy voice said from just inside the doorway. Ace swung a look. Clint Sinclair had stepped inside in time to hear Ace's angry outburst.

"It was talk like that, that nearly got the kid killed."

"I ain't afraid of Overstreet."

"Then that just proves you're sheep-dumb. Overstreet is the most dangerous man I know, except maybe for me."

"He ain't nothing but a worn out old man. I could take him easy."

"Just you hold on right about there. I don't reckon I have many I could call friends, but I count Hugh Overstreet one of them. Hugh is the second fastest gun hand I ever seen."

"And who would be the fastest?"

"Me. And you ain't even close."

"You've been aching to brace me from the first time we met, haven't you?"

"Now that you mention it, yeah, I reckon as how I have, at

that. Fact is, Bonham, I don't like you. You're a sneaky, back-shooting coward. I'd be doing the world a favor if I shot you right now."

As they talked both men squared off. Ace Bonham dropped into a gunfighter's crouch, feet wide apart, knees slightly bent, his hand only a hair's breath from the pistol tied to his leg.

Clint Sinclair casually brushed the edge of his long, black coat back, exposing the deadly-looking black-handled .44 in a hand-tooled buscadero belly holster. For a few deadly heartbeats they both hesitated, their gazes fixed, unblinking, on the opponent's eyes.

"Nobody talks to me like that, nobody!" Ace shouted as his hand streaked upward with a fist-full of pistol. It would be the last words he ever spoke.

Sinclair's hand moved with blinding speed, faster than the eye could follow. In one motion his hand swept the .44 from its holster, thumbed back the hammer as part of the same movement, and feathered the trigger.

His first bullet punched a hole in Ace Bonham's left shirt pocket. The second followed its companion no more than an inch to the right. The twin explosions in the confines of the saloon echoed around the room. The two bullets exited Bonham's back in twin geysers, showering blood over the bar and the floor behind him.

Bonham's eyes went wide in shock. His unfired pistol clattered to the floor. His face twisted in pain. He staggered backward with blood gushing between his fingers that gripped his fatal wounds.

His mouth opened wide in a silent scream, but all that came out was exiting air. He toppled over backward and landed with a soft thump and went still, staring at the ceiling with sightless, rounded eyes. His booted feet jerked with false life, for he was dead before he hit the floor.

# Chapter XXIII

Mary was up before dawn. It was Sunday. For some months now, it had become a regular weekly ritual that she and the children drive the wagon into town to attend Sunday church services.

She looked forward to these weekly outings. She received comfort from Reverend Hensley's messages, but it was more than that. She wouldn't admit it to the children, but she couldn't deny it to herself, she looked forward to having Sunday lunch with George.

If the weather was nice they usually picnicked down by the creek near the church, if not, they ate together at the café in town.

Mary busied herself in the kitchen, carefully packing the fried chicken, potato salad, and pumpkin pie that she had spent half the day before preparing.

Outside, she heard Shep barking as Ray Sawyer hitched up the team and wagon. *I better get the girls up,* she thought.

She hurried into the girl's rooms and shook them awake.

"It's time to get up, Marilyn," she told her oldest daughter. "We need to hurry, it's a long way into town and we don't want to be late for services. Get your sister up while I finish packing our picnic lunch."

"The Holly's and the Green's will be picnicking with us today won't they?" Marilyn asked.

"You mean will Caleb Green be eating with us, don't you?" Mary laughed. "Of course they will. I couldn't keep Caleb away if he was hog tied. I swear, I don't see what you see in that boy."

"Oh mother, I know you like him."

"Yes, yes I do. He's a fine young man. He'll make a wonderful son-in-law, *someday!*"

Mary returned to the kitchen. As she packed the items they would need for their picnic, she found her mind returning more and more often to George Paxton.

She enjoyed his company. She liked sitting next to him in church, feeling his nearness, catching his frequent sideways glances at her during Rev. Hensley's messages.

Her thoughts were scattered by Sally's loud vice from the bedroom.

"Mom, I can't find my other pink sock."

"Marilyn, would you help Sally find her sock."

Finally, everything was loaded into the wagon. A faint grayness lightened the eastern sky. Ray Sawyer helped them up into the wagon and handed Mary the reins. She slid their Henry rifle into the saddle boot strapped to the side of the wagon seat.

"There's biscuits in the oven, Ray, and the coffee's hot. We're staying in town tonight. We should be back by noon tomorrow."

"I'll be fine, Mrs. Littlejohn. You folks have a nice visit. I'll watch after things here."

"I know you will. I can't imagine how we ever got along without you before you came."

Mary popped the reins and the mules leaned into their harness. They were rested and ready for the long trip into town.

Just shy of eleven o'clock, Mary pulled the team to a stop under a big sycamore tree near the church. George was waiting for them.

"Good Morning, ladies," he greeted cheerfully.

"Morning, Mr. Paxton," Sally said happily, jumping down from the wagon and running to meet her friend Betty Jean.

Marilyn was already off the wagon and hurrying to meet Caleb Green.

George reached up to Mary to help her down from the wagon. Her foot slipped on the wagon bed and she fell into his waiting arms. Neither of them made an attempt to move.

Their eyes met, and held the other's captive for a long moment. Mary felt George's arms around her, holding her, their bodies pressed closely together. Her head spun. It felt good. In her entire life no other man's arms had held her like this except her late husband. How long they embraced neither knew nor cared. It was as if time stopped. They were alone. There was nothing else. There was no one else. All that mattered was here, now.

Somewhere in the vague, foggy depths of her consciousness, soft organ music and her daughter's voice shocked Mary back to reality.

"Mother, Services are starting."

Her face flushed red. She jolted from George's arms. Straightening herself and smoothing the imaginary wrinkles from her Sunday dress, she flicked a glance toward the front of the church where her daughter waited on the steps, then at George.

"I...I'm sorry, George."

"I'm not" He smiled. "You go on inside, I'll unhook the team and join you shortly."

The service was long, and Mary didn't hear a word the preacher said. Her mind was racing, her emotions confused by the morning's events. With blood burning in her cheeks she stole glances at the man sitting beside her. So close. She could feel the warmth of his nearness.

She became aware of George's hand against hers on the seat between them. Light as a butterfly's touch, yet the heat from it raced up her arm and straight to her heart.

Blood pulsed through her veins and flushed her body from head to toe. Never had she been more aware of her need. She heard her breathing become heavy and erratic. Convincing herself those around her could hear it too, she covered her mouth with a hand and glanced quickly around.

Suddenly the service was over. Mary hadn't even been aware of the closing song. Folks were shaking hands, exchanging pleasantries, and making their way slowly toward the door.

The weather was perfect for a picnic. The Greens' and the Hollys' joined and together, they all spread their lunches for a big dinner on the ground. There was lots of delicious food, laughter, and fellowship with good friends.

The afternoon ended all too swiftly. By mid-afternoon both the Holly and Green families had loaded their wagons and headed home. Marilyn and Caleb had a hard time parting. Caleb had to run to catch up with his family after lingering in his goodbyes with Marilyn.

George and Mary stood side by side at the end of the street and watched the wagons disappear in the distance.

Marilyn and Sally headed back to the Hotel. George and Mary strolled down by the creek. Both were silent as they walked together. Arriving at the creek bank, they sat down on the thick, green grass. George lazily tossed a small stick into the glassy water. They watched the ripples spread out in every direction.

"Mary, I've got to ask you something. Please answer me honestly, will you?"

"Of course."

"Am I just imagining things that aren't there, or did you feel something between us this morning by the wagon?"

"You aren't imagining it."

"You must know how I feel about you?"

"I know, George. And I feel the same way about you, it's just..."

"I don't mean to be rushing you, Mary, I mean, if you need more time?"

"It's not that, George. You're a wonderful man. Any woman would be proud to have you. It's Tad. I know he's doing what he feels like he has to do, but until this thing is settled, until he's back home safe, I just can't be what you would need me to be or what I would want to be. Can you understand that?"

"Of course I can. Thanks for explaining. We'll talk again when it's all settled."

"I'd like that."

They held hands on the walk back to the hotel. *It feels good,* Mary thought.

Marilyn and Sally were waiting on the boardwalk. They all had a relaxed dinner together. After dinner George told them all goodnight and headed for his office. Mary lay awake for hours, replaying the events of the day. *Maybe someday,* she thought...*maybe someday.*

After saying a prayer for God to keep Tad, Lupe, and Hugh Overstreet safe, she finally drifted off to sleep.

George felt like he was floating as he walked back to his office. He was light-headed and the wide smile on his face refused to go away. He couldn't remember a time in years that he had been so happy. *She cares for me. Mary actually cares for me, she said so.* He felt like pinching himself to make sure he wasn't dreaming.

After having a cup of yesterday's coffee, he blew out the lamp and sprawled onto the small cot in back that served as his bed. Since Hugh took off with Tad and Lupe he was without a deputy again so he slept in the office rather than riding out to his own home.

He lay awake for a long time, thinking about what a lucky man he was. Just the hope of one day being married to Mary was like a dream come true. The clock on his office wall said half-past one the last time he looked at it.

Somewhere a rooster crowed. Another answered and soon a chorus joined in to welcome a new day. George rose eagerly, knowing that he was having breakfast with Mary and the girls.

After washing up, shaving, and changing shirts, he headed for the hotel to meet them in the lobby. The sun was fresh born, but already gave promise of another beautiful day.

He didn't have long to wait. Sally was the first one down the stairs.

"Morning, Mr. Paxton," she greeted cheerfully.

"Good morning to you, Sally. My, you look beautiful this morning."

"Thank you."

"Good morning, Marilyn."

"Good morning, Mr. Paxton."

"How are you this morning, George?" Mary asked.

George looked up the stairway and saw her. Mary wore a dark blue work dress and a blue ribbon that tied her hair back Sun slanted through the front window and set her long, blonde hair ablaze.

He just stared speechless for a long moment.

"I'm...I'm fine, Mary. Did you rest well?"

"As a matter of fact, I did, thank you."

"Is everyone ready for a good breakfast?" George asked.

"I'm hungry," Sally offered. "Papa use to say he could eat a buffalo."

"He might near could too," George told her. "Your pa was a mighty fine man."

"I sure do miss him."

"I know you do, Sally, we all miss him."

The girls ran on ahead. Mary looped a hand around George's elbow and, together, they followed the girls up the street to the café.

It was mid-morning before they finally drained the last cup of coffee. Marilyn and Sally had long since gone looking for their friends that lived in town. George and Mary had talked nonstop.

"I really need to go, George. It's a long way back to the Littlejohn valley."

I know. I just hate for all this to end. It's been really nice."

"It has for me too. I'll look forward to your next visit for dinner."

"Then keep a sharp eye. I'll be coming soon. I'll go hitch your team and wagon."

A half-hour later as George stood in the street and waved goodbye to Mary and the girls, he felt like the luckiest man in Texas. But as he watched the wagon disappear in the distance a strange, worrisome feeling gnawed at his insides.

# Chapter XIV

A day passed, then two, and still neither Ace nor any of his other four men had returned from Alamogordo. *What could be happening to them?* Buck Slade wondered.

"Brad, take your brother and a couple of the hands into town. Counting Ace, five men have ridden into town in the last three days. None of them have come back. I want to know what's going on, understand?"

"We'll find out."

Tad and Lupe sat on a bench talking with the old liveryman as four riders rode into town, heading toward the livery. Tad saw Lupe tense and has face go hard.

"What's wrong, Lupe?"

His friend nodded a point with his head.

"Here comes trouble. Those men, they are Slade's men. The two riding in front are Slade's sons, Brad and Billy."

Tad swung a look.

The one on a golden palomino was obviously the oldest son. He rode tall and straight in the saddle. Tad judged him to be straddling thirty. He was of medium build, small waisted, and with wide shoulders and was clean shaven. He wore a light colored, flat crowned hat with the brim curled on the sides.

A walnut-handled pistol was tied snuggly to his right leg.

The man riding beside him was obviously the younger brother. No one seeing his face would forget it. T. J. had done a job on Billy Slade.

Somewhat smaller than his older brother, young Slade was something of a 'dandy' to Tad's way of thinking.

Dressed in black from head to toe, he would most likely cut a wide path with the girls if not for his face. His deformed and twisted lips and heavy scars would be enough to make anyone lose their breakfast.

He rode a prancing, solid black gelding with a silver studded Mexican saddle and martingale. Two, shiny, pearl handled pistols were buckled around his waist in twin, black holsters.

Instinctively, Tad reached a hand and drew his Henry rifle close, levered a shell, and rested it across his knees.

The riders reined up near the corral fence.

"Hey, old man, my horse picked up a gravel or something," the young Slade brother said. "See to it."

As he swung to the ground his gaze settled squarely on Lupe.

"You look familiar, Mex. Have I seen you before?"

*"Si,* you have seen me."

Billy Slade kept staring hard at Lupe as the old liveryman lifted the horse's hooves, one at a time, and inspected them. He went to his workbench and came back with a pry. Turning his back to the horse, he placed the gelding's hoof between his legs and pried out a small, embedded gravel.

"The horse will be fine now, señor."

All the while, young Billy kept staring at Lupe. Finally, recognition washed across his twisted face.

"Sure, you're the greasy little Mex that use to hang around town, ain't cha?"

"I use to live here."

"Well-well-well. Hey, big brother, you know who this kid is? He's the one that caused me all that trouble a couple of years ago. Got my face busted up."

"Come on, Billy, we got work to do."

"You done growed up, Mex, even wearing a gun and all. My, my, is that big pistol supposed to scare somebody?"

Lupe didn't reply. He just stared at the younger Slade brother.

"I owe you, Mex. You know how to get that pistol out of the holster?"

Still, Lupe said nothing. But out of the corner of his vision, Tad sensed, rather than saw, Lupe shift his feet slightly. He knew his friend was preparing for the worst. Tad slowly inched his trigger finger in place.

"You think you're a man?" Billy Slade's voice rose until he was shouting his challenge. "You ain't nothing but a greasy Mex, good for nothing but for licking my boots. Remember how you licked my boots, Mex? How'd you like to do it again? Yeah, I think you need to lick my boots again."

"Billy!" his brother shouted at him. "Leave the kid alone and let's go do what Pa sent us to do."

"No, stay outta this, big brother. I'm gonna tell you one more time, Mex. Get over here and lick my boots or I'm gonna kill you!"

Lupe stood unmoving, his legs spread slightly, his gun hand hung loosely by his side, his gaze fixed on young Slade's eyes just the way Hugh Overstreet taught him.

Tad slanted his own gaze away from Slade, and fixed the

three riders with a stare. They all sat their mounts, hands on their saddle horns.

Billy Slade's hand snaked down to his right-hand pistol. Just as he grasped the butt and began to pull it free a loud blast beside Tad sounded, then another.

Twin fingers of flame spat from Lupe's pistol. Two holes appeared in Billy's chest. He staggered backwards, propelled by the force of two .44-40 slugs from Lupe's pistol.

Tad swung his rifle up to shoulder and aimed the nose directly on the older brother's chest, hoping the older brother wouldn't buy a ticket in this dance. He was wrong.

The older brother grabbed for his pistol. Tad feathered the trigger. The blast from his Henry rifle blew Brad Slade out of his saddle. Tad levered another shell even as instinct screamed for him to move. He rolled to his right and came up on one knee just as a bullet splintered the post behind the bench he had just vacated.

Gun smoke from the shooter still clouded in front of the man's face as Tad triggered another shot. His aim was true and deadly. The man dropped his smoking pistol and reeled sideways from his frightened horse.

Tad heard two more shots from Lupe's pistol. He flicked a look and saw the fourth man double over, then topple to the ground.

A pall of blue gun smoke hung like a cloud over the livery yard and stung Tad's nose. Before the smoke cleared, Hugh Overstreet, Sinclair, the bounty hunter, and Marshall Short all hurried up, their pistols in their hands.

"What happened here?" The Marshal demanded.

The old liveryman hobbled up.

"Young Billy drew down on Lupe because he wouldn't lick his boots. Lupe shot him slick as a whistle. When the older brother and the others took it up, Tad and Lupe killed 'em."

"Ain't been nothing but killing since you boys hit town, think I better hold on to your guns till you ride out."

The remark awakened Hugh's bad temper.

"Now just hold on there a minute, Marshal." Hugh said, "Maybe you didn't hear the livery fellow. He said the Slade boys drew first. That makes it self-defense. The boy's got the right to defend himself. You take our guns, you gonna take the Slade bunch's guns too?"

After a moment of contemplation, Marshal Short grudgingly relented.

"All right, you can keep your guns, but something's gotta stop all this killing. The town councils on my back and when Buck Slade hears about this, there's gonna be hell to pay."

"All the more reason, taking our guns ain't the answer."

A crowd of town's people had gathered. Women took one look, gasped, and hurried away. Men murmured among themselves.

"Some of you boys get these bodies over to the undertaker's," Marshal Short ordered. "The rest of you, go on about your business, ain't nothing more to see here."

"We'll be over at Sadie's if you need us," Hugh said. "Come on boys, we've got some talking to do."

The four walked up the dusty street, with Overstreet and Sinclair on either side, the two boys in the center.

Tad rested his Henry rifle across a shoulder. Townspeople stopped, watched the four, and then whispered something to those standing nearby.

Sadie poured them coffee as they scraped out chairs and sat down.

"Well, won't be long now," Overstreet said, blowing steam away from his cup and chancing a quick sip. "When his boys don't show up, Slade will be riding hell bent for leather into town with every gun hand that rides for him. You can lay odds on it."

"How we gonna play it?" The bounty hunter asked. "Four of us against fifty are mighty big odds."

"Yeah, too big. Somehow we've got to cut those odds down to size. Any ideas?"

"How you think he'll come in, scattered or in a bunch?"

"My guess is he'll come riding hard and fast and bring everybody he's got."

"I reckon," Sinclair said, aiming a look at Overstreet. "What about this McKenzie fellow and his Cattlemen's Association, think they'll fight?"

"Maybe, be worth a try. I'll ride out to his place and have a talk. Watch out for the boys until I get back."

"Seems to me they do a pretty good job of looking out for themselves."

Hugh rode north. At the end of the street he circled the giant oak tree and heeled his horse into a ground-eating short lope. As he rode his mind raced.

*How long did they have before Buck Slade found out about the death of his sons? Would he try to hold Tad and Lupe individually responsible, or would he take out his rage on the whole town?*

One thing for sure, even *with* the Cattlemen's Association, they had one heck of a fight on their hands. He had faced stiff odds before, but never like this. Without McKenzie and his men, Hugh knew they didn't stand a chance.

The sun was straight overhead when he rode through a gate and passed under a sign that read 'Lazy K". He passed two herds of fat cattle before spotting the ranch house in the distance.

A big barn, bunkhouse, and corral stood only a short distance from the house. The house was a dogtrot style made of heavy logs with a breezeway through the middle. Smoke from a noonday fire gave it a comfortable, homey look.

Alan McKenzie stepped from the barn and walked to meet him.

"Glad to see you, Overstreet. Come on in the house, wife was about to set the noon meal. Hope you'll join us?"

"Mighty nice of you, but I'm in a bit of a hurry. We need to talk"

"Of course, come on in the house, we can talk there."

Hugh followed the rancher into a den and folded into the armchair McKenzie indicated with a nod.

"What's on your mind, Mr. Overstreet?"

"Both of Slade's boys were shot and killed today in town. It's just a matter of time before word gets back to him. I figure when it does, he'll come looking for blood."

"No doubt about it. Who killed them?"

"Two boys, one sixteen and the other seventeen. One of them was the Mexican kid that grew up here, the other was T. J. Littlejohn's boy. Billy Slade was riding the Mexican boy pretty hard. Told him to get down and lick his boots or he was gonna kill him. Turned out he bit off more than he could chew."

"That Slade boy has been asking for it for a long while, looks like he finally met his match."

"Yep, the thing is, Buck Slade's gonna come riding in with everything he's got. I figure he's got maybe forty gun hands left riding for him. There's four of us to face him. We could use some help."

"You got it."

McKenzie rose and went to the door and stepped out on the porch. He took out his pistol and changed ends with it, then struck a shiny bell hanging from a rope. A loud ringing shattered the stillness.

Within seconds cowboys came running and riding from every direction. Hugh counted fourteen in all.

"Slim, I want you to ride hell bent for leather to the Thompson place. Tell Ben Thompson to gather his riders, arm them, and meet us in town as fast as he can.

"Bart, ride and tell Jack Young the same."

"Ray, you take the Hicks spread."

"Have them all send riders to the other ranches. Tell them to burn leather and meet us in town. Now ride!"

The three cowboys jumped into their saddles and lit out at full gallop.

"Eleanor, fetch my shotgun and a box of shells," he hollered.

But his wife was already a step ahead of him. She was standing there behind him with a sawed off Greener and a box of shells.

"The rest of you boys saddle up. We've got snakes to stomp."

Luper Long was the town drunk. He lived alone in a rat-hole shack outside town. He happened to be sleeping off a hangover out behind the livery when all the shooting woke him.

Peeking through the slats of the horse stalls, he recognized the two Slade brothers lying in pools of their own blood. Luper might be a drunk, but he wasn't one to miss an opportunity if it presented itself. He saw one in the deaths of the Slade brothers.

His whiskey soaked mind told him that Buck Slade might just be grateful if somebody come and told him what had happened to his sons, might even give him a few dollars for such important information.

Stumbling on shaky legs, he made it back to his place and put a bridle on old Jesse, his slat-ribbed mule. It took him three tries before he was able to climb into the saddle and stay on. Finally, he kicked the mule in the flanks and headed to the Slade ranch at a trot.

* * *

Buck Slade was concerned. It was nearing sundown and his sons still hadn't returned. He paced the floor, emptying glass after glass of whiskey. *Why was it taking so long?*

On every trip around his den he stopped at the window and gazed off into the distance toward town. *I should have gone myself*, he told himself again and again.

Finally, a single distant speck appeared, soon joined by four Slade outriders. Buck hurried to the veranda.

As the riders drew near, Buck felt disappointment gnaw his insides. *Who is this tramp? What is he doing here?*

They reined up near the hitching rail.

"Mr. Slade, this old geezer says he's got some important news you'll want to hear. He won't talk to anybody but you. We thought it best to bring him in."

"Who are you and what kind of news could you possibly know that I'd be interested in?"

"I'm Luper Long, Mr. Slade. I got some news about your two boys."

"What? What about my two boys? Let's hear it!"

"Well, sir, I reckoned as how the news I got might be worth something."

"Yes, yes, what about my boys? You'll be paid."

"Be better if'n I got my pay first."

Losing his patience with the old drunk, Buck dug into his pocket and withdrew a ten dollar eagle coin and dropped it at the man's feet.

Bending over and almost falling, Luper picked up the coin and stuffed it into his pocket.

"Your boys are both dead. Shot deader than a doornail at the livery in town. The other two with them are dead too."

Shock, disbelief, panic, all surged through Buck Slade.

*Dead? My boys dead?* A scream was born somewhere deep in the pit of his stomach, raced up his throat, and erupted into the deepening twilight.

His hired hands heard it and come running from every direction.

"Mount up!" He bellowed." I want every man armed and in the saddle in five minutes! They've murdered my sons! We're gonna burn that town to the ground along with everybody in it!"

# Chapter XV

Except for the heat, the ride back to the Littlejohn Valley was a happy occasion. The sweltering, noonday heat made the trip long, hot, and hard. The big team of Missouri mules plodded along as Mary and the girls laughed, sang songs, and laughed some more.

They had just topped a slow rise when she saw them.

Off in the distance, still only obscure specks on the prairie. Mary shielded her eyes and squinted. It was three horses, and one carrying two riders. They were heading toward Mary and the girls.

"Probably nothing to worry about, but riders coming," Mary said as she picked up her Henry rifle, levered a shell, and laid it across her knees.

The closer the riders got, the more concerned Mary became. She knew trouble when she saw it and these men were trouble. They were saddle tramps. Their clothes were nothing more than filthy rags. The horses they rode were slat-ribbed and looked like they would drop dead at the next labored step.

The one out front looked to be the oldest of the four. He was a big, swarthy fellow with a hawk nose and bloodshot, whiskey eyes. He wore a full, shaggy beard that was discolored with long present tobacco stains. Most of his front teeth were missing. His black, floppy hat was pulled down low, partially hiding his evil looking eyes.

Her best guess was that the other three were his sons. They reined their three horses up straddling the road. Mary had no choice but to rein her team down.

"Afternoon, to you, Ma'am, hot day ain't it?" The leader said, his whiskey soaked voice gravely and rough.

In reply, Mary offered only a small nod

"Where you ladies be headed?"

"We're on our way home from town. May we get by please?"

"Dangerous for three purty ladies, way out here in the middle of nowhere all by yourselves."

"We're not by ourselves. Our men folk are back there a ways, they'll be along directly."

"You don't say?" The man said, standing in his stirrups and shielding his eyes to sweep the flat prairie with a searching gaze. "I can see for miles but don't see no men folk, reckon maybe they got lost or something?"

"They'll be along. Now, may we get by, please?"

"Don't appear to me they *is* any men folk,." he said. "Fact is, Ma'am, we got ourselves a little problem here. Jubal there, his horse just plumb played out a ways back, truth is it wasn't much good anyway, but now ole Jubal is having to ride double with my youngest boy, and they don't gee-haw atall."

While the older man was talking the other rider walked his horse around the team of mules and was approaching Mary's side of the wagon seat. Panic spiraled through her.

"Please, don't come any closer," she pleaded, lifting the Henry rifle and pointing it at the dirty and sneering young man.

The man just laughed an evil-sounding laugh and sneered defiance. His hand shot out and grasped the barrel of the rifle. Mary squeezed the trigger. The rifle roared. Marilyn and Sally screamed.

The bullet tore the man from his saddle, but his grasp on the barrel of Mary's rifle was strong and it was ripped it from her grasp as he tumbled to the ground.

"What'd you do?" The father yelled. "You done shot my boy!"

The old man scrambled from his horse and dropped to the ground beside his fallen son. He cradled the boy in his arms, rocking back and forth lifting his face to the sky and moaning loudly.

The remaining two slid off the single horse and climbed up onto the wagon. One of them grabbed Mary and flung her roughly to the ground, the other shoved Marilyn off the other side.

Mary landed with a jolt. Her breath left her. She gasped to catch her breath. The world flared hot and bright before her eyes. Her head spun crazily. Pain radiated from her left shoulder and ripped apart sight and sense. She felt herself slipping into unconsciousness.

*No!* Her mind screamed at herself. *I can't! I have to stay awake to take care of my girls. I have to!*

"Oh, Ike, my boy, she done killed you," the man wailed. "I'm sorry, son. I'm sorry. She'll pay, son, she'll pay for killing my boy."

Mary stared through glazed eyes as the evil-looking man dropped his son's head to the ground and pushed to his feet. He stumbled toward her with hatred burning from his eyes.

A rumbling growl erupted from his twisted, filthy mouth.

A hand reached out, grabbed her by the hair, and yanked her to her feet. She saw the fist coming straight for her face. She felt the impact. She heard the sickening crunch. Pain exploded from her cheek and jaw. Her head snapped back. Sparks flared and dimmed before her eyes. Her legs buckled. The world went black.

Blackness. Mary blinked her eyes. It was still dark. Her head ached. She licked at her lips and tasted her own blood. *Am I alive or dead?*

Blinking her eyes into focus she tried to raise her hand to her mouth but found that both hands were tied behind her back. Her ankles were also tied.

*Where am I? What's happened? Where are Marilyn and Sally?*

She tried to turn her head. It hurt. Light from a dying campfire cast weird shadows. Through the dim light she saw Marilyn nearby, tied to a wagon wheel. She tried to move but found that she too, was tied to one of the wheels of their wagon.

*Sally, where is Sally?*

Mary tried to twist her head to look at the wagon wheels behind her, but couldn't. Memory of the earlier events began to return. *Those men, the shooting. The man hit me. How long have I been unconscious?*

Shattered, hollow, raw, Mary somehow reached into the depths of her being and summoned strength she would need to face whatever lay ahead of them. Mary twisted her head in her daughter's direction.

"Marilyn," she whispered through split and swollen lips. "Marilyn, can you hear me?"

"Yes, are you all right, Mother?"

"I'm all right. Where's Sally? Do you know where Sally is?"

"She's all right. She's in the wagon. They tied her up too."

"Did they hurt you? Did they...?"

"No, they didn't hurt me. What are we going to do?"

Tears blurred Mary's vision. She waited for her heart to stop pounding in her throat, for her legs to stop quivering. She thought about her daughter's question for a long moment before answering with a shaky breath.

"I don't know. Lord help me, I don't know."

Morning came slow. Mary hadn't closed her eyes since she regained consciousness. Through the haze of her own pain, she had searched her brain for something, anything, which might get them out of this tragic situation, but found no answers.

By the time dawn's first rays lightened the eastern sky the father of the boys was up and stoking the fire to life. They had, of course, found the supplies Mary had bought at the store in town. From somewhere, they had produced a small, blackened coffee pot and was filling it from a canteen.

Glancing over at Mary, he lumbered over and squatted only inches from her. He stared at her for a long moment, his eyes so filled with hatred she shivered at his glance.

"See you're awake. Good thing. You don't pull your share of the load I got no use for you. You or the girls give me trouble or try to run, I'll let the boys have you first, and then I'll cut your throat. You hear me?"

Mary nodded.

Reaching around, he untied her hands.

"Now get up and rustle us up some breakfast and be quick about it."

"I could do it faster if the girls helped."

He thought on the suggestion for a minute. Without a word he walked over and untied Marilyn's hands and feet.

"The little one stays tied up."

"We need a moment for private time."

"What's *private time?*"

"You know, the natural functions of the body."

"Oh, well, best get to it. Ain't much *private* out here on the prairie."

Marilyn came over and helped her mother up. They checked on Sally. She was asleep. Mary looked at the area where they were camped. There was nothing but flat prairie, no trees, no bushes anywhere around. How were they going to preserve what little dignity they had left out here on the prairie? It was still dusky dark so the far side of the wagon would have to do.

With what little supplies were available, they managed to put together flapjacks and salt pork for breakfast. The three men gobbled it down like it was good.

"What are you going to do with us," Mary managed to ask while they were eating.

"Been thinking on that," the grizzled old man said. "Lost the wife awhile back, God rest her soul, and every man needs a woman. You ain't bad to look at, might need some meat on your bones but you'd do. About decided when we get back to our place we'll get hitched all proper like."

"You gonna marry her, Pa?" The one they called Jubal questioned. "You'd just beat on her till you killed her like you did our ma."

"Now you hush your mouth, boy. You show some manners to your elders. Your ma sassed me, that's why I had to hit her. A man needs to keep his women toeing the mark. You best learn that. They learn to like it after awhile."

Mary's breath snagged in her throat. *Marriage?* The thought made her skin crawl. *I'll die before I'd marry him!* She sucked in a ragged breath and tried to quell the flood of fear and disgust that washed over her.

She became suddenly afraid she was going to cry, that she wasn't strong enough or wise enough to deal with what had befallen them. But she realized that she couldn't show weakness in front of her daughters, she had to be strong for them.

*Think. I've got to think. Will someone realize we are missing and follow? George will, I'm sure of it. But how will he know where we've been taken. A trail, that's it, we've got to leave signs for him to follow.*

"Besides, I see you keep eyeing up that golden haired one. We might have to let that preacher say words over you and her at the same time."

Jubal cackled an evil laugh and slanted a stare at Marilyn.

"Yeah, Pa, I'd shore like that. I shore would."

Mary heard her daughter gasp.

"We got to get moving," the big man said. "Load our stuff in the wagon, woman. Boys, hitch that mule team and let's get rolling, it's still a long ways to our mountain."

While loading the wagon, Mary managed to tear a small piece off her petticoat and weigh it down with a rock.

They rode all day headed due west. Mary came to the realization they were headed toward New Mexico Territory. She had never been there, but from what she remembered from conversations with T. J., they had to be getting close to the border.

She learned that their captors were the Isoms. The father's name was Amos, the older son was Jubal, the one she had shot was named Ike, and the young one, who was deaf and dumb, was named Carlyle.

Several times during the day, on the pretext of checking a wheel or using the bathroom behind some bush or tree, she left small pieces of her petticoat, either tied to a bush or weighted down with a rock.

Just before sundown they spotted a small shack up ahead. It was made of adobe and a thin tendril of smoke trailed from the chimney. A nearby corral held a single horse.

"Well, would you lookee here?" Amos Isom said, "The

good Lord has done provided us with a horse way out here in the wilderness. He surely does work in strange and mysterious ways. Jubal, ride around back and make sure nobody gets out that way."

*What are they going to do?* Mary wondered. *It sounds like they mean harm to whoever lives there.* A tight, dry knot of fear coiled just beneath her ribs. Panic shot through her. *Should I call out and warn them?* Then the evil man's threat rang in her mind, *'You give me trouble and I'll turn you and the girls over to my boys and after they get through with you, I'll cut your throat.'* She clamped her hands tight on the mule team's reins to still the trembling.

The youngest brother had been riding the tailgate of their wagon. At his pa's motion he jumped off and ran to the side of the small house, pulling a long knife from his belt as he ran. Jubal reined his horse around the house and disappeared.

"Hello the house,." Amos Isom hollered.

"What you want?" A voice from inside answered.

"Mind if we water our stock from your well?"

"Water's free."

"Mighty neighborly of you, friend."

"Ain't your friend. Water and move on."

"Mr. Isom," Mary whispered, "please don't do this."

"Hush your mouth, woman," Isom warned from the corner of his mouth.

"If'n I wasn't a God fearing man, I might take offence, neighbor. We mean no harm. Just want to water our stock and pass the time of day."

This time there was no answer from inside, only murmured arguing that Mary couldn't understand. A long minute passed. The heavy front door opened slowly. The twin barrels of a shotgun peeked through, followed by a shirtless man with dirty britches and suspenders. He looked to be somewhere straddling fifty. He was mostly bald headed, and wearing week old whiskers.

The face of a frail looking woman could be seen over his shoulder.

"Howdy to you, neighbor," Amos Isom greeted cheerfully. "We're obliged for the water."

"Welcome to it. Never turn down a God fearing man."

The farmer took a few steps toward Isom and lowered the barrel of his shotgun. That was his final mistake. Without so much as a pause, Isom reached under his coat, drew a pistol, and shot the man in the chest.

Marilyn and Sally began screaming and couldn't stop. Mary sat wide-eyed, stunned and speechless by the cold - blooded killing.

The man's eyes went wide. He dropped the shotgun and clutched at his chest, trying vainly to stem the flow of life-giving liquid down his bare chest. He collapsed to his knees, and then toppled over onto his face in the dusty ground. It all happened in the space of a few seconds.

Inside the house a woman screamed. Young Carlyle saw the killing and raced around the corner of the house and burst in through the closing door. Another pitiful gurgling scream shattered the stillness. Then silence.

*Deathly silence.*

Carlyle emerged from the house holding the long knife. The blade was dripping blood.

George Paxton clamped his hat on his head and took a sweeping look around the office. Satisfied that he had done everything he needed to do for the day, he walked outside and closed the door behind him.

Swinging a look to the west he squinted at another beautiful Texas sunset.

*Reckon I'll mosey over and grab a bite of supper.* He headed that way.

A rider galloping down the street drew his attention. He recognized the rider as Ray Sawyer, Mary's hired hand, and knew immediately that something was wrong.

Ray reined his mount to a sliding stop and hit the ground breathless.

"Sheriff, something's bad wrong. Mary and the girls ain't back yet."

"Ain't back yet? Today is Wednesday. They left here before noon on Monday."

"She told me before she left they would be back Monday. At first I figured she decided to stay over another day, but when she still didn't show up today, I got worried."

"See any sign on the way in?"

"Didn't look. I rode as fast as I could to tell you."

"Round up some men. Bring Wolf-cries-in-the-night, the tracker. Hope we don't need him but I want him there just in case. Catch up as quick as you can. I'm riding that way."

Even as he spoke he wheeled and was running for the livery. As he saddled his gray, he told Silas Isaac what was going on. "Catch me another fast mount for an extra and saddle it for me, will you? Bring it to up to the office. I need to grab my rifle and a few things before I head out."

"You betcha," the old liveryman said, hurrying to do what George had asked.

Within short minutes George was galloping North with a long-gaited bay on a lead rope behind him. His heart was in his throat. *What if something bad has happened to Mary and the girls?* His lips set in a hard line and he lashed the gray to greater speed.

Darkness outran his horse, and gradually the faint, two day old wagon tracks disappeared into the gathering blackness. A thin sliver of moon couldn't have come at a worse time, there was barely enough light to ride by, let alone track two day old wagon prints.

He reined back his mount to a slow walk, leaning far over in the saddle in order to barely make out the tracks.

Another mile and he was forced to get off and walk. He was afraid the wagon had veered off the road at some point. He couldn't afford to miss where they left. *I can't give up,* he told himself. *If I have to wait until morning, that's another night Mary and the girls are in danger. I've got to keep going. I've got to find them.*

Finally, caution would allow him to go no further. He was forced to make camp, wait for the others, and daylight in order to continue. He led his horses off the road a few feet, and scrounged up enough wood to build a small fire to chase off the chill of a Texas night.

Taking his small coffee pot from his saddle bag, he filled it with water from one of his canteens, dumped in a handful of coffee, and set it on a couple of rocks over the fire.

George sat with his head down, staring blankly into the fire. When the coffee had come to a boil he took a tin cup from his saddlebag and poured it full of the steaming black liquid. He blew away the steam and took a sip. The coffee was hot enough to scald hide off his tongue. *It's my fault. I never should have let them make that trip by themselves.*

The time was near midnight when the posse reached George. They reined up, climbed down, and started stripping saddles from their tired horses before gathering around the campfire. George raised his tin coffee cup in a howdy.

"Find anything, George?" Reverend Hensley asked.

The sheriff was quiet for a time before answering.

"No, too dark to trail. I figure, for whatever reason, they must have left the road somewhere, and we can't take the chance of running past it. Hate to, but its best we wait until first light."

George let his gaze sweep around the group gathering around the fire. Wiley Stubblefield was there, so was Ray Sawyer, Mary's hired hand. Jed Holly and Homer Green and his son, Caleb stood close by. Wolf-cries-in-the-night stood a ways off from the others.

George walked over to him.

"I'm obliged to you for coming, friend."

"Me want to help find woman and little ones."

"We'll get started at first light."

The Indian tracker nodded.

"Can't imagine what could have happened to them, just to disappear into thin air like this," the storekeeper said.

"They wouldn't have gone off on their own," George said, returning to the fire.

"You thinking somebody kidnapped them then?"

"That's the way I got it figured."

"We'll find them. We won't stop until we do."

"Well, may as well roll out your bedrolls and get what sleep you can. Gonna be a long night."

Before first light the posse was up and in the saddle. The trail was now three days old and the shifting wind had all but erased the faint wagon tracks. The Indian tracker took the lead on foot and had no trouble following the trail at a crisp jog.

George put two men a hundred yards on either side to ride parallel to the road just to make sure they didn't miss the tracks if they left the road.

It was mid-morning when they found what they were looking for. An untrained eye would have completely missed it. Wolf-cries-in-the-night squatted in the road. He pointed here and there, reading the signs as a white man would read the newspaper.

Three riders had intercepted the wagon. There was a fight. Someone was wounded. The Indian pointed to a faint brown spot on the ground.

George knelt for a closer look. No mistaking what it was, it was blood, but whose?

"Sheriff, over here," Homer Green shouted. "Looks like a grave."

The words stabbed George's heart. He felt the air in his lungs go stale and thin. His hands went cold, his stomach churned wildly as he headed toward them. *Oh dear God, please don't let it be Mary or one of the girls.*

It was a grave, right enough, shallow by the looks of it, one dug in haste. Rocks had been piled on top to discourage wild scavengers. The only question was, whose grave was it? George wasn't sure he wanted to know.

Several men fell to their knees, scooping handfuls of dirt aside. George closed his eyes and breathed a silent prayer. As the diggers scratched closer to the body in the grave a silence followed, lengthening.

# Chapter XVI

Just past sundown Hugh rode into Alamogordo flanked by McKenzie and a dozen of his riders. Shadows were lengthening. They reined up at the Ace High saloon and dismounted.

Sinclair, Marshal Short, Tad and Lupe pushed through the door and met them on the boardwalk.

"So, your thinking Slade will come tonight?"

"He'll come," Hugh told him. "And it ain't likely to be pretty."

"We've got more help coming, Marshal. My riders are out rounding up the other ranchers right now."

"Maybe I can talk some sense into Buck's head," Marshal Short said. "Maybe it won't come to shooting."

"Don't bank on it, Marshal," Sinclair said. "I've seen his kind before. Like Hugh said, he'll come, and he'll come with killing on his mind. All talking is gonna do is get you shot."

"Well, can't see as it'll hurt anything, I don't reckon."

"Best get these horses off the street, Mr. McKenzie," Hugh said. "Might want to have the boys take them down to the livery."

"Good idea. You heard him, boys."

Each man slid his rifle from saddle boots. Two of the men gathered the reins and led the horses down the street to the livery.

Over the course of the next two hours half a dozen ranchers arrived with their heavily armed men. McKenzie guessed they now had over fifty fighting men ready and willing to face Buck Slade and his hired guns in a final showdown.

Hugh Overstreet emerged as the natural leader. Accepting his role, he gathered his forces together and laid out his plan. Men were disbursed to every rooftop, every window and every doorway in town, with orders not to fire until Hugh gave the order or in the event Slade's outfit rode in shooting. They were free to fire at will.

With everyone in place, things were set as well as they could be under the circumstances. They settled down to wait.

"Here they come!" Someone on a rooftop yelled.

A rumble of galloping horses sounded from both the North and the South. They were attacking from both directions. Clouds of churning dust could be seen rising in the gathering darkness.

Hugh stood in the door of the saloon. Tad and Lupe punched out the windows with the nose of their rifles and levered shells into the chambers. Marshal Short foolishly stood in the middle of the street with a shotgun cradled in the crook of an arm. *The fool is about to get himself killed,* Hugh thought.

As the first wave of horsemen charged into town from the North, Hugh saw the torches carried by each rider and knew their meaning. They intended to burn the town.

"Fire!" Hugh shouted over the thundering hoofs and triggered a shot at the lead rider.

A volley of rifle fire sounded. Riders tossed their torches through windows and onto rooftops as they charged down the street.

Marshal Short ran for cover, firing his shotgun at the oncoming riders as he ran.

Tad put his sights on the rider of a hard-charging bay at the front of the attack. His muscles tightened. His hands made sweat on the rifle stock. He followed the fast moving rider just a bit, and then nudged the trigger. The rifle slammed into his shoulder and the explosion made his ears ring.

The bay swerved as the rider's weight shifted to one side. His body slid off the side of his mount, his torch and rifle flying from his hands. He hit the dusty street and tumbled over and over, finally coming to a stop and not moving.

Up and down the street rifles popped. Charging riders were swept from their horses in the hail of bullets from every direction. Tad, Lupe and Hugh were firing, levering a fresh shell, and firing again.

Rider less and wide-eyed horses trailing their reins, some with saddles hanging to the side, shied this way and that trying to avoid downed riders and escape the flames. Tad found a fresh target, but just before he squeezed the trigger a shot from Lupe's rifle sounded and Tad's target was ripped from the back of the fast running horse.

A bullet shattered a piece of remaining glass from the window only inches from his face. Another dug a notch from the window sill. He swung the nose of his rifle and found the chest of a second rider. He feathered the trigger and tore the man from his saddle, arms askew, and hands clawing empty air.

Up the street, buildings were ablaze. Huge flames licked their way toward rooftops. Glowing, red-orange sparks lifted from the fire and disappeared into the ink-dark sky. No one dared attempt to fight the fires because of the battle raging.

Just as Tad thought the fight was over, a new wave of attackers charged into town from the south. He knew Buck Slade would be riding the magnificent black stallion and searched vainly for him among the riders, but to no avail. The object of his hatred was nowhere to be seen.

The torches and fires lit the street as if it were day. Tad could clearly see the galloping horses with flaring nostrils, their manes flying in the wind as they raced up the street. He brought his rifle to bear on the nearest target. His Henry Rifle jolted his shoulder. The man grabbed his chest and somersaulted backward from his saddle.

A noise behind him made him crook a look over his shoulder. Two men had slipped into the saloon through the back door. Their pistols were in their hands and rising for back shots.

Hugh and Lupe must have heard the noise too. Before Tad could react with his rifle, Hugh and Lupe whirled, drew their pistol, and shot the attackers. The face of the man in front mirrored surprise and then sudden pain as he dropped his pistol and grabbed at his chest. The second attacker was blown over backwards by shots from both Lupe and Hugh at the same instant.

The battle raged for what seemed an eternity, but in reality, lasted only a few minutes. As suddenly as the attack had begun, it ended. The street was strewn with the dead and dying. Rider less horses galloped aimlessly back and forth, nickering to one another, obviously confused by the battle and the fires raging all along the street.

Men began to emerge cautiously from rooftops and doorways, their guns ready for any threat.

Hugh, Tad, and Lupe pushed through the bullet- splattered door onto the boardwalk. Marshal Short had somehow survived his earlier foolhardy efforts and stepped out of a nearby alleyway.

Everyone jumped in and helped save as many buildings as they could. Several were too far-gone to save. When they had done all that could be done, they gathered in the street.

"Did anybody ever spot Buck Slade?" Hugh asked.

"Never saw hide nor hair of him," McKenzie replied.

"Well if that ain't a fine howdy-do," Sinclair said, walking

up. "He sends his men to die but he hides in a hole somewhere.
I'll find him."

"Not unless you beat me to it," Hugh told him.

"He back-shot my pa," Tad spoke up. "He's mine."

"The Cattlemen's Association will find him. He can't hide
from us," McKenzie said. "All of you, just back off. Slade burned
the town. Jurisdiction or no jurisdiction, nobody burns my town.
I'll handle it."

Lupe just smiled and said nothing.

"Well, we've got a lot of burying and cleaning up to do,"
Marshal Short said. "We best get at it."

They worked all night. The wounded were treated and jailed
for trial. The dead were gathered and come daylight, were buried
in the graveyard outside town. All told, thirty-eight of Slade's
men were killed, and twelve sat in jail awaiting trial. Only two
of the Cattlemen's Association riders were killed and three
wounded, but they would recover.

Ladies of the town cooked and served food for the weary
men who had fought, then worked to save and clean up their
town. When mid-morning came everyone was worn out and
found someplace to lie down for awhile.

The hotel had somehow escaped serious damage. Tad,
Lupe, and Hugh dragged themselves up the stairs to their rooms
and fell into their beds with their clothes still on.


Tad and Lupe awoke to someone banging on their door.
They blinked themselves awake and were surprised to discover
it was already morning . They had slept nonstop for most of
eighteen hours.

"Tad, this is Hugh, you and Lupe best come take a look."

They both jumped out of bed, embarrassed they had slept

that long. Hurriedly dressing, they rushed downstairs. Hugh was waiting for them in the lobby.

"What is it?" Tad asked. "What's happened now?"

"Step outside and take a look for yourself."

They both hurried through the door and onto the boardwalk. A small crowd was beginning to gather at the end of the street near the giant oak tree. A man hung from a rope tied to a strong limb that stretched over the road. His hands were tied behind him. A magnificent black horse stood rider less nearby.

Tad glanced, first at Lupe, then at Hugh.

"Is that—that Buck Slade?"

"Seems so."

They headed toward the growing wad of folks. Clint Sinclair, the bounty hunter, stood nearby. Marshal Short and McKenzie hurried up.

"Who...who hung him?" The lawman asked.

"Wish I could say it was me," Sinclair said, "but it weren't. From the looks of these prints, I'd say just one man done it."

"Why would somebody go to all that trouble?" the lawman wondered aloud. "A bullet would have been easier."

"If I was guessing," the bounty hunter said, "I'd say it was somebody looking for revenge and wanted to send a message."

Tad and Lupe stood a ways off. Each gave the other a quick, sideways glance.

The marshal turned to face Hugh Overstreet, his gaze obviously searching for answers.

"Know anything about this, Mr. Overstreet?"

"Nope."

"What about you, McKenzie? You or your men have every reason to hate Buck Slade, you have anything to do with this lynching?"

"Had nothing to do with it but can't say I'm all broke up over it either."

"We gonna cut him down or let him just swing in the breeze?" Sinclair asked.

"Go ahead," the marshal said, "help me cut him down."

Sinclair stepped forward, pulled a long hunting knife from a belt scabbard, and before the lawman could reach out to catch the body, slashed the rope just above Slade's head. The body made a heavy thump when it hit the ground.

"I was gonna catch him," Marshal Short commented, frowning at the bounty hunter.

"Didn't see no need, seeing as he's dead."

"Hard way for any man to die," The lawman said.

"Ain't no easy way," the bounty hunter replied.

# Chapter XVII

Mary and the girls were in shock at what they had witnessed. The senseless slaughter of the innocent farm couple sent little Sally into a deep, silent trance-like state. Marilyn couldn't stop crying and Mary brooded silently. *These aren't men,* Mary thought, *these are animals, predators, like a pack of wolves.* The brutal horror could never be erased from their minds.

The wagon had been abandoned at the farmhouse. Mary rode one of their mules and Marilyn and Sally rode the other. With the horse stolen from the farmer, the Isoms now each had a horse.

Their little caravan was strung out in a line. Amos led the way with the girls next, then Mary, with Jubal and the younger Isom following closely.

"Making better time without the wagon," Amos called over his shoulder to his boys. "Couple more days we'll be home."

Mary could imagine what *home* to the Isoms would be like. She just prayed someone would follow and rescue them before they reached wherever it was they were going.

She knew it would be harder to follow horses than wagon tracks so she determined to try to leave more clues than she had before. The problem was they seldom stopped.

Spotting a clump of bushes up ahead, Mary decided to make a try.

"Please, Mr. Isom," she begged. "The girls and I need to stop for a few minutes."

"You women are all alike, always complaining bout something or other. We'll stop but you better hurry."

"We will. Thank you."

Mary reined her mule toward the bushes. Marilyn did the same. They slid off their mules and hurried behind the thick stand of bushes.

"Hurry, girls," Mary said, tearing off a piece of her petticoat and tying it to a bush.

They emerged from the bushes and climbed onto their mules just as Amos reined up. Mary tried to divert his attention by asking a question. She didn't want him finding the piece of cloth she had tied to the bush.

"How much further is it to your home?"

Amos ignored her question and reined his horse around the bushes. He spotted the piece of cloth and yanked it from the bush. Ruthless, icy fingers of fear clutched Mary's heart.

"Figured you was up to no good," he bellowed.

He reined his horse beside Mary's mule, his big hand lashed out, backhanding Mary and knocking her to the ground. The blow stunned her and rattled up her neck and made her limbs go weak. Her stomach churned. She fought for breath. Darkness swooped in and out. She blinked her eyes, desperately trying to bring the world back into focus. Dazed by the vicious blow and jolted by the fall, she lay there, on the verge of losing consciousness. She licked her lips and tasted salty tears mingled with blood.

"You'll learn to mind me, woman!" He shouted, sliding from his horse.

A big foot lashed out and landed against her side. Excruciating pain like she had never known shot through her. All the air rushed from her lungs. She doubled up from the kick. "You'll walk the rest of the way."

Taking a rope from his saddle, he made a loop and placed it around her neck and drew it tight. As he remounted, he wrapped the loose end around his saddle horn.

"You fall, I'll drag you!"

As Isom heeled his horse the slack came out of the rope, jerking Mary to her feet. She stumbled forward, still stunned by the blow, the fall from her mule and the kick. The world around her spun crazily. Sharp pains from her side throbbed through her. She hurt all over. Tears welled up. Useless tears. Tears that did no good. She choked them back, impatient with herself for her self-pity. She drew a long and painful breath and struggled forward, one stumbling and labored step after another.

Marilyn sobbed uncontrollably, completely overwhelmed with everything happening and obviously knowing she was helpless to help.

Little Sally rode silently behind her sister, arms wrapped tightly around Marilyn's waist, a blank stare fixed straight ahead.

Time lengthened. As the day wore on Mary grew weaker and weaker. Her legs felt leaden. She stumbled with every step, not knowing where she could find the strength to manage the next step. Her mind told her to give up but her heart refused to obey.

Her legs gave way and she fell. The rope went taunt and tightened around her neck. Isom's horse paused with the added weight. He jerked a look over his shoulder and kicked his horse in the flanks, forcing it forward.

Somewhere, far away, Mary heard a scream and recognized it as her daughter.

Marilyn leaped from her mule and rushed to grab the rope with both hands, tugging on it against the horse's strength.

"Please, in the name of God, stop! You'll kill her!"

Ignoring the girl's pleas, Amos continued forward, pulling both the woman and the girl. Marilyn's heels slid in the dirt, trying vainly to ease the rope's pressure on her mother's neck. She screamed, pled, and prayed.

Finally, Isom pulled his horse to a stop and stared at the girl for a moment before speaking.

"See to her."

Marilyn rushed to her mother's side. She fell to her knees and loosened the rope from around Mary's neck and cradled her mother's head in her lap.

"Water, I need some water," she screamed.

"We'll stop here for the night," Amos said, tossing a canteen onto the ground beside the girl.

She quickly picked it up and loosed the cap. Lifting her mothers head, she poured a few drops onto Mary's dry and cracked lips. She bathed her mother's face.

It took a few minutes before there was any response. Finally, Mary's dry tongue licked at her cracked and bleeding lips. Her eyes fluttered weakly, and then closed again. Silent tears seeped from the corners and tracked into her dirt-caked hair.

"Mother, can you hear me? Take a small swallow."

Mary felt as if she were floating on a soft cloud. From somewhere far away a familiar voice was calling, so faint, so far away. In her confused mind she saw T. J. standing far off in a swirling fog. His arms were outstretched toward her, beckoning for her to come to him.

"Mother, please wake up, please!" A faint voice called.

Closer, the voice was getting closer. Mary fought to recognize the voice. She felt a touch on her face, soft, loving, familiar. She struggled to tug her eyes open but kept slipping back into the blackness that had its arms wrapped around her, cradling her in its softness, refusing to let her go.

Marilyn Littlejohn became a woman in those moments, there, kneeling on the ground beside her mother. She was changed from a young, naïve, teen-ager, dependant upon her mother for strength and guidance, to a woman.

She watched her mother's face. She listened to the ragged breathing. She, somehow, deep inside her soul, was aware of the life and death struggle being waged by her mother before her very eyes.

She leaned over and pressed her cheek to her mother's face. She caressed her mother's cheek with loving fingers. She pressed her lips to her mother's eyelids with kisses as light as a butterfly's touch.

"Please, mother, please don't leave us. We need you."

From somewhere, somewhere deep inside Mary's soul, she tapped a new source of strength. A surge of life raced through her, filled her, and refreshed her. Her eyes fluttered open.

Marilyn was there, hazy at first, but then came into focus. The love and concern Mary saw in her daughter's eyes was beyond measure. She lifted one corner of her swollen, cracked lips into a thin smile.

"Oh, thank God," Marilyn whispered. "You're awake. I thought..."

Mary nodded her head and reached a weak hand to touch her daughter's.


George Paxton didn't breathe as the last few handfuls of dirt were raked away from the body.

"It's a man," Caleb Green said, then repeated his words, his voice higher pitched and happy. "Looks like he was shot."

The sheriff let out a long sigh of relief. He bent close as they brushed dirt away from the man's face, and a feeling of recognition wrinkled the lawman's forehead, something about that face seemed familiar.

He searched his memory, mentally thumbing through the stack of wanted posters like he had done a hundred times before. Suddenly the face flashed before him. But the face in that grave was only one of four faces on the poster. The name, what was the name?

Then he remembered. Isom. This boy was one of the Isom clan, wanted far and wide for everything one could imagine and many things that no one could imagine. They were a bad bunch, a real bad bunch.

*If the Isom clan has Mary and the girls, God help us, we've got to find them real quick.*

"That fellow is one of the Isom clan," George told the men crowded close for a look. "Amos Isom is the pa. He has three sons. Looks like just two now. They're the worst of the worst. Law's been looking for them for years. No one knows where they live, or even if they got a regular place they call home. They turn up now and again, go out on a robbing and killing spree, then crawl back into whatever hole they crawled out of.

"Looks as if they've got Mary and the girls. If we don't find them real quick, odds are we won't fine them at all, least ways, not alive. It may already be too late."

He paused and swung a look at the men gathered around the fire.

"I'm giving every man here fair warning, I'm gonna follow this bunch to hell and back if need be, but I'm gonna find them. Any man that wants to turn back, I'll understand. You've all got wives and families to take care of.

"No telling how long this will take. It will take as long as it takes. There won't be no turning back, no quitting. If you want to pull out, now's the time. Sorry to put it to you that way but that's the way it is."

Without so much as a sideways glance George rose and walked to his gray horse and toed a stirrup with his left boot. Once aboard, he tightened the lead rope to the bay, lifted the reins, and gigged his horse into a short-lope.

He was aware of a rider coming up behind him, but didn't look back to see who it was. Didn't matter, he was going even if no one went with him. He had to find Mary and the girls before it was too late. Finally, Wolf-cries-in-the-night rode up beside him, nodded and pulled his appaloosa ahead to follow the trail.

Another horse pulled up, then another, it was Homer and Caleb Green. George slanted them a look. They nodded.

"Good to have you along."

"Wouldn't be nowhere else," Homer said.

"Me either," Caleb agreed.

The Indian tracker found the small piece of cloth Mary had left, before noon. George's heart leapt at the sight. *Most likely Mary's idea,* he thought. *That means she knows we will be following.*

Circling buzzards ahead sent a chill racing up George Paxton's spine, and a lump lodged in his throat. They spiraled in lazy descending circles like a beacon, pointing the way to death. George and the Greens topped a slow rise and spotted the farmhouse. Wolf-cries-in-the-night was already there.

A horde of the black scavengers sat on top of the remains of a corpse in the front yard of a remote farmhouse. They fought one another in bursts of flapping wings and clawing talons for the opportunity to tear at the corpse with their razor sharp beaks.

What once had been a man was now nothing more than bloody bones with remnants of flesh clinging to them. The scavengers darted in, ripped a piece of flesh from the skeleton, then retreated to devour their meal.

As George and the Greens rode into the yard the buzzards reluctantly hopped a safe distance away and fixed their big eyes on the intruders, waiting impatiently until they rode away so they might return to their feast.

Caleb took one look and jumped from his saddle, unable to make it around the corner of the house before losing the contents of his stomach.

Noticing the big birds coming through the partially open door of the house, George knew another body was inside. He stepped down from his mount and pushed on the door, and quickly stepped back. Half a dozen of the scavengers beat a hasty retreat through the open door, their legs carrying them through the door and into the yard before their big wings lifted them into the air.

It wasn't a pretty sight. The woman, whoever she had been, wasn't recognizable even as a woman except for the bloody dress that had been ripped and torn to shreds by the buzzard's sharp talons. George breathed a silent prayer. *Thank God it isn't Mary or one of the girls.*

"See if somebody can locate a shovel," the sheriff said, emerging from the cabin. "We need to bury what's left of these folks."

While Homer and his son were digging graves to bury the farmer and his wife, George and Wolf-cries-in-the-night read the story of the signs.

The Isoms had abandoned the wagon, having stolen the single horse that had been in the corral. That was bad news. That meant they could now move faster and that meant it would take longer to catch up to them, and that was bad news indeed.

George swiped his hat from his head and swatted his leg with it in disappointment.

"Let's help them with those graves," he said to the Indian

tracker, "we've got to get as far along as we can before dark catches us."

The four worked feverishly, and finally, the bodies lay in shallow graves and covered with rocks. They were all glad to leave the place of death.

Darkness closed in. Still they followed the faint trail left by five sets of hoof prints. As the darkness thickened, they walked and led their horses until the trail was swallowed by the night and completely disappeared.

They unsaddled their horses and cared for them before spreading their bedrolls and lying down to catch a few hours sleep. Tired as he was, George couldn't sleep. He kept picturing Mary and the girls in the hands of killers like the Isom clan. It hurt his heart to think what they might be going through even that very minute.

# Chapter XVIII

There was but one topic of conversation in Alamogordo that day: who hung Buck Slade? Every man in town had their own idea, but no one knew for sure. One thing everybody could agree on, they were all glad he was dead.

Clint bid them all, adios, and rode out by mid-morning. McKenzie and his Association friends followed a short time later. Hugh, Tad, and Lupe decided to take the day and rest up before facing the long ride back home to Lubbock, Texas.

Marshal Short and the town council met that afternoon. The lawman found Hugh and the boys at Sadie's eating a thick beef steak and all the trimmings. He scraped out a chair and sat down without a word. Only after his first sip of coffee did he acknowledge their presence.

"I want to apologize to you fellows. Seems I'm always misjudging you Texans. You boys have done our little town a big service and the town council wanted to show their appreciation.

"Far as we can tell, Buck didn't have any kin, least ways any that is still alive and would own up to it. They don't know what will happen to his ranch, land, and cattle, but they wanted Tad to have that black stallion. It's down at the livery. It's all yours, son, and here's a proper bill of sale. We sure feel bad about your pa and we're grateful that you got rid of Buck for us."

"But marshal," Tad objected, "I didn't . . ." His words were cut off by the lawman raising his hand.

"It's over and done, son. You don't have to explain nothing to nobody."

Tad just ducked his head, shaking it slowly from side to side.

Hugh and Lupe looked at one another and shared a thin smile.

Morning found Mary feeling some better. At least she could walk, though barely. Every bone in her body hurt. She had an ugly, purple rope burn around her neck from being dragged. Her lip was split and swollen. Her face was black and blue and one eye was swollen completely shut.

But Amos Isom must have had a softening of heart during the night. He told Marilyn to help her mother get on her mule. By first light they had already finished a cup of morning coffee and were in the saddle.

Their surroundings changed drastically that day. The flat, seemingly endless prairie gave way to rolling foothills. Up ahead, Mary could see high mountains, reaching their lofty peaks toward the powder-blue sky.

She knew Amos Isom would be watching and that she wouldn't have a chance to leave any more trail markers for whoever might be following.

By mid-morning they came upon a clear mountain stream that rushed down out of the mountains and meandered out into the prairie behind them.

"We'll water," Amos Isom said, reining up and stepping off his horse.

Mary and Marilyn quickly helped Sally down from the mule and splashed water in their faces. Sally still didn't respond. Mary was worried sick about her but there was little she could do at the moment.

"Do we dare try to get away?" Marilyn whispered to her mother.

Mary remembered what Isom had told her about trying to escape and shook her head.

The stock slaked their thirst and the canteens were refilled. Mary felt somewhat refreshed after the stop. She still hurt something awful but the cold water eased the hurt some.

All afternoon they climbed steadily, weaving along a faint mountain trail. From the ease with which they found their way through the rocky trails and canyons, it was apparent the Isoms were in familiar territory.

*That probably means they are getting close to their home, whatever home would be for a filthy bunch like them. How will anyone ever find us now?*

The further they went, the more discouraged Mary became. She decided that they couldn't rely on the hope that someone would eventually follow and perhaps even find them, she had to plan for the worst. She had to find a way for them to escape, if possible, or to defend herself and her daughters.

Just before sundown they broke out of a little canyon into a long, narrow valley. One side of the valley was steep, nearly straight up. A fresh, clear stream ran the entire length of the valley.

The other side sloped gently for a ways, then climbed steeply and became a sheer flat mountain face. A sturdy log cabin stood on the sloping side of the stream. A thick grove of large pine trees served as a backdrop for the cabin. A small barn and pole corral straddled the stream, a short ways downstream from the cabin.

The yard was cluttered with piles of junk and trash. Hides of several different kinds of animals were stretched on racks and were covered with flies, feasting upon the remaining bits of rotted meat still clinging to the hides. Mary would have thought a filthy bunch like the Isoms would have lived in a cave somewhere, not in a beautiful spot like this with a sound log cabin.

"You women get in the house and rustle up some supper," Amos ordered gruffly.

He and the boys took the reins and led the horses to the barn to strip them of their saddles. Even as they walked away, Mary saw Jubal casting long, sideways glances at Marilyn.

Mary said nothing but it added another worry to an already long and growing list in her mind. They hurried to do as they were told. They had already learned the consequences of incurring Amos Isom's wrath.

They could smell the place long before they opened the door. The stench of body odor, rotted meat, and urine was unbearable. When they opened the heavy door the putrid air from inside almost knocked them down. They both held their noses and ducked inside.

The cabin had only one main room with a small lean-to room attached to the back. Four makeshift bunks hugged three of the walls with a rock fireplace occupying the fourth wall. There was no stove but a blackened kettle hung over where the fire should be.

Filthy clothes and trash was ankle-deep. There was so much litter in the lean-to one couldn't even get inside. It was piled waist high.

"How can anyone live in a pig sty like this?" Marilyn asked, still holding her nose.

"We aren't, not even for one day," Mary said, letting her gaze sweep the room. "Start carrying it all outside and dump it into a pile. We'll burn everything that we can move."

Mary found it difficult to talk. Her lip was split and her entire face was swollen. Her throat hurt something awful where the rope burn was. But she willed herself to put her pain out of mind and concentrate on keeping her girls from further harm.

They went to work. Sally stood in a corner and stared blankly. Armload after armload was gathered, carried outside, and piled up. Soon, the pile was head-high and growing.

On a trip outside with her arms full of discarded clothes Mary bumped into Amos Isom who stood blocking the doorway.

"What you doing, woman?" he roared like a wounded bear.

Mary swallowed the lump in her throat and summoned the courage to have her say. She decided if it took another beating then so be it. Anger flushed her face and filled her voice.

"You can live like a hog if you want to but don't expect me and my girls to live like one.

"We're cleaning this place up. You can help or get out of the way."

For a long minute he just stood staring hard at Mary. Then abruptly shrugged his shoulders and stepped aside. She felt like she had just won the Civil War. She decided to press her luck and stay on the offensive.

"If you want to help, set fire to that pile of trash yonder and send one of those sons of yours to kill us something to eat. The other one can help carry out this trash."

He just gave her another hard look and ordered the two boys to help them. He picked up his rifle without saying another word and walked toward a stand of trees upstream.

The fire was roaring. Flames leaped high into the darkening sky. Secretly, Mary was praying the smoke might be seen from a long distance hopefully by George Paxton or whoever might be searching for them. She felt certain someone would come.

By the time everything that wasn't attached to the cabin had been carried out and burned, a single rifle shot was heard from upstream.

Mary gave the two boys buckets and sent them for water from the stream. When they finished, she asked them build a fire in the fireplace. She had Jubal cut her a long pole and then tied a large rag to it with rawhide strips to make a mop.

She found three large cowhides stretched on racks outside and spread them on the dirt floor of the lean-to. She intended for her and the girls to sleep there. At least by sleeping together they would have to fight her to do harm to the girls

By the time Amos returned with a deer slung across his shoulders, the wooden floor of the cabin had been scrubbed clean with some lye soap she had found. Satisfied that the cabin was now at least bearable, Mary and the girls went down to the creek and took their time washing themselves, using the soap they had found. It felt good.

Isom and the boys skinned and dressed the deer and brought her a large chunk of the fresh meat. Mary cut it into smaller pieces and soon had deer stew simmering in the pot over the fire.

The cabin smelled better. The offensive odor hadn't been completely removed, but at least it was now bearable. The aroma of the deer stew began to waft through the cabin. After eating almost nothing for the last three days, the food smelled delicious.

The Isoms must have smelled it too and came tromping into the cabin. Mary met them at the door and planted herself squarely in the middle of it.

"You'll go wash up in the creek before you'll set at my table," she announced firmly.

Isom took a hard look at her, anger flared in his eyes for an instant, and then, without a word, he turned and headed for the creek. The boys followed.

Even under the circumstances, everyone seemed to enjoy the meal. Sally managed to eat some but she still stared unseeing, lost somewhere in a world of shock and denial, seemingly unaware of what was going on around her. Mary was deeply concerned for her daughter.

The looks the oldest Isom son was now giving Marilyn were increasingly more open and obvious. Mary knew trouble was brewing, it was only a question of when it would come. She just hoped whoever was following them arrived before the showdown came.

While cleaning up after supper, Mary slipped a sharp hunting knife into the folds of her dress. She knew it wouldn't help much, but at least it was something she might be able to use to defend the girls in case it came to that. She had found a worn and tattered Indian blanket and managed to tie it over the doorway to the lean-to room. Now, without a word, she and the girls went into the lean-to and pulled the blanket over the door behind them.

Mary placed herself between the girls and the door, fully prepared and determined that they would have to kill her before anyone harmed one of her daughters. She lay there, listening to sounds from the outer room, alert for any hint of trouble, gripping the handle of the knife with a sweaty hand.

Soon, the angry muffled voices ceased and the snoring began. Mary began to relax, secure in the belief that the expected showdown would not come that night. At some point her need for sleep overcame her weary and pain racked body and she drifted off to a troubled sleep.

They were saddled and moving before grayness tinged the eastern horizon. Far ahead, George could see the distant mountains and knew they had already crossed the border into New Mexico Territory.

Wolf-cries-in-the-night heeled his appaloosa into a long trot. George and the Greens did the same. The ground passed quickly under the beating hooves. The Indian tracker suddenly reined to a stop beside a thick clump of bushes. He slid off his horse and walked a circle around the bushes, then squatted on his haunches.

"Big man beat woman. She walk behind horse. She hurt plenty bad."

The news was like a mule's kick in the stomach to George. His throat was suddenly as dry as sand. Muscles in his jaw throbbed. His lips set in a thin line and his eyes went hard and mean.

"Is she gonna make it?"

"She walk."

Remounting, they moved on toward the mountains. The Indian kept his dark eyes fixed to the ground. He kept George informed as to the woman's condition. Wolf-cries-in-the-night pointed to the footsteps.

"Woman weak, she stumble."

Farther on he pulled his horse to a stop and pointed at the ground.

"Woman fall. Man drag woman behind horse."

The words spoken by the Indian tracker emptied George Paxton's soul. Icy fingers seized his heart and wrung it dry. Grief pressed up the back of his throat. Guilt gnawed at his conscious. Anger as he had never known before swept over him like a tidal wave. His muscles taunted as tightly as a bowstring.

"Slow and hard," he breathed quietly. "I swear it, Isom, I'm coming for you and you'll die slow and hard."

# Chapter XIX

Before the roosters crowed, Hugh, Tad, and Lupe swung into their saddles and bid the old hostler *adios*. Here and there yellowish patches of lamplight filtered through windows as the riders made their way out of town.

The big black stallion was on a lead line behind Tad's big buckskin. He still couldn't believe the town had given him the magnificent animal.

"What do you plan to do with the stallion?" Hugh asked as they rode.

"Been thinking on that," Tad answered. "Reckon he'd sire some high-bred colts, so about decided I might start raising horses."

"Sounds like a mighty fine idea. No doubt about it, that's the best looking piece of horse flesh I ever laid eyes on. Tell me something, son, how'd you do it?"

Tad swung a quick sideways glance at Lupe, then back at Hugh Overstreet.

"What do you mean?"

"How'd you manage to string Buck Slade up all by yourself?"

"I told you, I didn't do it."

"Yeah, I know what you told the marshal but you ain't got me convinced."

"Then I reckon nothing I could say is liable to change your mind. Would it make a difference if I had?"

"Not in the least."

"Then it don't matter, does it?"

"Likely not."


By noon they were winding their way through the foothills of the Sacramento Mountains. It took most of the day to pick their way through the heavy timber, gorges, and rocky mountain passes.

As shadows lengthened and the sun disappeared somewhere behind the mountains, they made camp in a clearing beside a rushing stream. After supper they banked the campfire against the chill of mountain air and settled down to enjoy another cup of coffee.

Nobody talked much to speak of, mostly sat quiet, staring into the fire, each one lost in their own thoughts. Lupe broke the silence.

"Mr. Overstreet, how long does it take to get over killing a man?"

"Don't know, son, I'm still working on the answer to that myself."

"How many men you killed?"

"More'n I want to talk about. Killing ain't something to be proud of or go around bragging about. A man does what he has to do, no more, no less. You're a hand with that pistol, Lupe, maybe the best I ever seen. You've a natural skill, something no one can teach another, your eyes are quick and you're a good judge of distance.

"But all that can be both a blessing and a curse. I'm not saying you will go looking for trouble. Trouble will come looking for you soon as word gets around, and it will. I heard talk back in Alamogordo already by folks telling how fast you are with a gun. Just want to say, both you boys done good back there in town, you fought better than most men."

Tad thought on what Hugh said, but it didn't seem like it needed a reply. Instead, he listened to the sounds the wilderness makes, wind blowing through the tall pines, the lonesome call of a coyote, the gurgling sound of the mountain stream rushing over the rocks. He heard all these sounds, listened, and thought of home.

It lacked an hour before daylight when they packed their gear and stepped into the saddle. It was clear that Hugh was as anxious to get back to Lubbock as Tad and Lupe were.

The sun rose high and hot. By noon they had left the mountains behind and broke out onto the flat, desert-like plains. They rode steady and quiet, eyes alert for any sign of trouble.

By mid-afternoon they came upon the Rio Penasco River. It wasn't much by way of a river, narrow, shallow, and muddy-colored, but it was a welcome sight to both men and horses.

After filling their canteens and letting their horses slake their thirst, they climbed in their saddles and pointed the noses of their horses northeast.

By mid-day the country had become even harsher. In times long past rivers had cut deep gouges in the desert like some giant snake winding its way across the land, but now those rivers had long since dried up leaving only the deep scars behind. Rock strewn hills forced many detours.

Hugh pointed to the sky.

"Keep a sharp eye. Watch the flight of the birds. They'll lead us to water."

Sure enough, they all seemed to be headed in the same direction. The riders reined their mounts that direction too.

Following the flight of the birds they swung down into a deep canyon and followed it for a few hundred yards. Up ahead the canyon pressed close together to form a small opening.

"Let's ride right easy like," Hugh told them, "Might be other folks looking for water got here ahead of us."

They rode with their rifles propped against a leg, ready for whatever might come. Riding through the opening, they saw flocks of birds watering at a small pool of water near the end of a box canyon. As the riders approached the birds lifted to flight.

"Let's water up and get out of here," Hugh said. "I've got the jitters about this place."

In minutes they had filled their canteens, watered the horses, and were headed back out of the canyon.

That's when they saw them.

A wad of mustang ponies clogged the entrance to the canyon in front of them no more than two hundred yards away. Perched atop each pony was a Comanche warrior. The Indians spotted them at the same time and were as surprised as Hugh and the boys.

"Comanche," Hugh said as he sawed his horse around. "Take cover."

Tad swept the area behind them with a quick look and found cover in a jumble of fallen rocks, some larger than a wagon, with an opening large enough to hold their horses. Wheeling the buckskin he reined it and the black stallion into the opening in the rocks and dismounted before his mount came to a sliding stop.

Lupe followed him in and leapt from his saddle. Hugh and their pack mule, Solomon, weren't far behind. Each found a firing position behind the rocks and was pleased to see that their position gave them a clear field of fire of the narrow opening.

The Comanche recovered quickly. The chilling war cries filled the canyon and turned Tad's blood cold, gooseflesh pimpled along his spine. The thunder of mustang hooves on the rocks that littered the canyon floor sounded like there must be a hundred or more of them.

"Here they come!" Hugh shouted, bringing his rifle to shoulder.

The Comanche charged through the narrow canyon opening at full gallop. Because of the narrowness of the opening, only four or five horsemen could pass through at once. Hugh, Tad, and Lupe laid down a heavy barrage of fire and left the first wave of mustangs rider less.

Still they came.

Tad's sights fell upon a big warrior's chest. He squeezed the trigger. The Comanche spun crazily from the back of his horse. Tad levered his Henry and swung his sights to another target. The screaming Indian had two large feathers woven into his hair. His mouth was wide open. Tad's .44 slug tore away half of the savage's face. The warrior somersaulted over the rump of his pinto and landed disjointedly in the dirt, dead before he hit the ground with a bullet to the head.

The Indians were slow to learn and continued to charge through. A bullet brushed past Tad's ear so close he felt the wind from it, and then ricochet off a boulder and whined off into the air.

Their shrill war cries echoed along the confines of the canyon. Again, the deadly accurate fire from Tad and his companions cut them down, leaving dead or dying Comanche scattered along the canyon floor.

Because of their sheer overwhelming numbers, inevitably a few managed to get through and charge their rock stronghold on foot. The warriors were upon them, screaming and running headlong at them with war clubs upraised.

Tad dropped his rifle and scooped up his two sawed off shotguns lying at his feet. With a flick of his thumbs, he drew back all four hammers. He swung one shotgun up and fired point blank into the savage faces of three oncoming Comanche.

The force of the blast sounded like a clap of thunder in the canyon. Like a swarm of deadly hornets the double-aught pellets tore through flesh and bone, ripping, tearing, and leaving nothing in their wake except mangled flesh and death.

A muffled cry escaped one warrior's lips as the boiling buckshot tore into him, lifted him off his feet, and sent him flying backwards, his arms flailing and hands clawing the air for something to hold onto.

The explosion jarred Tad to the bone. His ears rang and his teeth rattled. Tad winced when he saw the result of his shotgun blast but strangely felt no remorse, knowing the Indians would have killed them in a heartbeat. *It's a horrible thing what a shotgun can do to a man though*, Tad thought.

The battle ceased. A strange, eerie silence settled over the canyon.

"Reckon what they're up to?" Lupe asked.

"Never know about a Comanche," Hugh told them. "If I was to venture a guess, I'd say they're trying to figure another way to get at us."

"Maybe they'll just go away."

"Not likely. They saw our horses. To a Comanche, a horse is what gold is to a white man, especially that black stallion. Ain't a Comanche alive that wouldn't die to own a horse like that."

"Then what do you think they'll try?"

"I'd say they're looking for a way to get above us. I saw a few rifles among them. If they could get up on top of that rim up yonder, they could cause us some hurt."

"I could climb up the side of the canyon and be waiting on them," Lupe suggested.

"Not unless you can sprout wings," Hugh said, staring at the rim above their heads. "Doubt if a lizard could make it up that rock face."

"I could."

"It's too dangerous. One slip and that would be all there was to it."

"Got any better ideas?"

Hugh chewed on that for a spell. He had to admit his young Mexican friend was right, there just wasn't much of anything they could do.

Without waiting for approval, Lupe reached down and shucked his boots and socks. He took a coiled lariat rope from his saddle and slipped it over his head and shoulder.

"When I get up I'll throw down one end of the rope. Tie my rifle to it and I'll hoist it up."

"You mean to climb barefooted?" Hugh asked.

"*Si,* When I was young I use to climb the rocks near Alamogordo."

"Well, good luck to you, Pard. Hope you know what you're doing."

Hugh stood guard with his rifle as Tad walked over to the canyon face with his friend. Tad lifted his head and gazed upward at the sheer face of the cliff. He could see no way in the world anyone could climb that.

"Sure you want to do this, Lupe?"

"If there is a chance it will save my friends I would gladly give my life."

Tad couldn't stop the tears that welled up in his eyes. A knot crawled up the back of his throat and threatened to choke him. He pressed his lips tightly together to choke back a sob.

They hugged.

Then, without a word, Lupe turned and started his climb.

Feeling the rock face with searching fingertips, he somehow

found tiny cracks, crevices, and protrusions that were invisible to the eye. He used his fingers to hold his weight and his bare toes to move his body slowly upward.

Inch by inch he moved higher and higher. Tad held his breath. Hugh glanced over his shoulder continuously. He had never been much on prayer but suddenly found himself asking the Man upstairs to give his young friend the strength to make it to the top.

Some sound, some feeling, something woke Mary. She jerked upright to a sitting position. It was dark. Her head twisted to take in her surroundings. Only then did she remember where they were.

"What is it, Mother?" Marilyn whispered beside her.

"It's okay, honey, guess I just had a bad dream. Go back to sleep."

Marilyn turned over and pulled the single blanket tighter around her throat. Mary lay awake, listening to every sound. Loud snoring could be heard from the other room.

A hand went to her aching side. She felt gingerly along her ribs but felt nothing that seemed broken. She hurt all over. It took every effort she could muster just to breathe.

Assessing their situation, she knew it was unrealistic to believe that Isom and his boy, Jubal, would hold off long before enjoying the company of her and Marilyn. Someway, she had to find a way for them to escape before that happened, but how?

False dawn slanted in around the blanket covering of the lean-to room. As quietly as she could, she slipped from under the blanket and ducked through the doorway.

Isom and his two boys were still snoring loudly. She tiptoed across the room, meaning to slip out the front door and wash herself in the stream while she still had a little privacy. Halfway across the room she stopped. Lying on the floor beside Isom's bed was his pistol and holster.

*If I could get my hands on that pistol, we might have a chance,* she thought.

Without considering the consequences, she changed directions and inched toward the sleeping giant. She held her breath, afraid the sound might alarm the cruel man. Her heart pounded. Her pulse quickened.

With only a few feet to go, her foot stepped on a squeaky board. Instantly Isom's eyes slammed open. He sat upright and stared straight at her.

"What you doing?" He demanded.

"I, I was going to make some coffee."

He stared at her suspiciously for a long moment, then picked up his boots and stomped into them.

"I'll need some fresh water," she said, picking up the water bucket and heading toward the front door.

She hurried down to the stream and filled the bucket. Glancing over her shoulder at the cabin and seeing no one, she knelt beside the cool stream and washed herself as best she could without undressing.

She was halfway back to the cabin when Isom came through the front door. He paused and watched Mary walk toward the house. His gaze on her felt evil and made her skin crawl.

"I'm sending Jubal for the preacher today."

The news struck Mary in the pit of her stomach. She wanted to throw up. The very thought of marrying a filthy pig like Isom revolted her.

"When will he be here?"

"Hard to say, day, maybe two."

Mary said nothing more. She pushed past him and walked into the cabin. *A day, maybe two, that means we don't have much time left. Whatever we are going to do we can't wait.*

Isom must have woke the boys because they were both up, at least in body, Jubal sat on the side of his bunk with his head in his hands and his eyes still closed. Carlyle, the deaf and dumb one staggered around the cabin looking for his boots.

Mary took notice that both of their holsters and pistols was still lying on the floor beside their beds.

*Tomorrow morning,* she told herself. *I'll try again tomorrow morning.*

# Chapter XX

George Paxton rode with his shoulders slumped. His hopes were fading fast that he would be able to reach Mary and the girls in time to save them.

Wolf-cries-in-the-dark pushed onward at a killing pace. His pinto was a rangy mustang that could set a gait and maintained it for hours on end. George's dappled gray began to fall behind. Homer and Caleb were far behind and struggling to keep up.

They were in the mountains now. Tall pine trees reached toward the sky and scrub cedar gathered in thick groves to clog the way. Deep waterways carved out by untold centuries slowed their progress but still the Indian tracker pushed on.

Darkness was falling fast. George kept one eye peeled to the deepening darkness and the other fixed on the tracker. Finally, the Indian reined into a small clearing and slid off of his pinto.

"We camp here."

George considered protesting, pleading that they push on, but then realized that the Indian knew what he was doing.

They made camp, built a small fire, and made fresh coffee.

It was boiling by the time Homer and Caleb Green rode wearily into camp. After they saw to their horses, George sliced some salt pork into a pan and Homer opened a jar of beans from a tow sack he had tied behind his saddle.

After supper they poured another cup of coffee and settled back against upturned saddles to relax. Only then did Wolf-cries-in-the-night share the news with them.

"Not far now."

George thought he hadn't heard the Indian right. He wrinkled his forehead and lowered his tin cup, staring at the tracker.

"What did you say?"

"Not far now."

"What do you mean? How do you know?"

"They know trail, been here many times."

"Then you're saying we might catch up to them tomorrow?"

"Tomorrow."

The news lifted George's spirits. He nodded. Thought about the Indian's promise, then nodded again. His thoughts settled again on Mary, as they had since the moment Ray Sawyer rode into town. He stared into the flickering flames of the campfire and silently prayed that God would see fit to watch over them until they could reach them.

It took awhile. Sometimes Lupe spent long minutes searching for a handhold before burying his torn and bleeding fingers into a faint crack and inching himself upward.

Finally, his hand clamped onto the top of the rim and he pulled himself over the edge. Both Tad and Hugh let out long sighs of relief.

Lupe tossed down the end of the rope and Tad tied his friend's rifle to it. After the weapon was pulled up, Lupe lifted a hand and waved.

The sun was fading fast over the canyon. Twilight set in. Still there were no signs of the Comanche. Tad began to tell himself that they had pulled out, that Lupe's dangerous climb had been for nothing.

His thoughts were short lived.

From high above Lupe's rifle barked, then again. A warrior plunged over the edge of the Canyon wall. As he fell he let out a chilling scream that ended abruptly when his body hit the bottom. His rifle clattered on the rocks beside him. The blood-curdling scream reverberated along the canyon, and before it died away another shot from above sounded.

"Sounds like Lupe is taking care of business," Hugh said.

They waited. Darkness settled over the canyon. No more shots from Lupe's rifle were heard.

Some soft sound jerked their attention to the narrow opening. Fleeting shadows appeared seemingly out of nowhere. The Comanche were upon them.

Tad glimpsed a dark shadow hurtling through the air toward him. He threw up one of his shotguns and fired point blank. The weapon belched fire and death. The attacking warrior was caught in mid-flight by the heavy shot and literally blown apart. Blood and bone fragments splayed across the rocks around them.

Nearby, Hugh fired his pistol. The roar of his gun ripped through the settling silence. A stab of orange flame pierced the darkness. A soft slapping sound testified that his slug had found its mark. A deep grunt confirmed it.

Two of the enemy scrambled over the protecting rocks in front of Tad. He saw their snarling faces in the dim moonlight an instant before triggering a load from his shotgun.

Another raced screaming through an opening in their rock barricade. Hugh whirled and shot the savage twice in the chest.

As quickly as it had started, it ended. If there were other Comanche inside the opening, perhaps only scant feet from where Tad and Hugh waited, they were either trying to wait them out or they simply disappeared like vapor.

First one, then the other hunkered down behind their protective rocks to reload their weapons, their nerves stretched taunt, their gazes sweeping the darkness, waiting for the next attack.

They waited.

The night crept by slowly and still they didn't hear a sound. Finally, they decided to alternate watches so at least both could catch a little sleep.

Morning finally came. Apparently the Comanche had decided that no horses were worth the price they had already paid. They had pulled out sometime during the night.

Venturing out cautiously from behind their rock fortress, they were shocked to find not a single Comanche body. Those left alive had somehow gathered up their fallen brethren and taken them away.

Lupe appeared on the rim of the canyon above their heads and lifted his rifle over his head. Tad and Hugh did the same.

"We'll meet you at the mouth of the canyon with your horse!" Tad shouted to his friend.

Lupe nodded his head and headed that direction in a jog.

All day long Mary laid her plans of escape.

Just as Isom had said, he sent Jubal riding off just after sunup with orders to return with the, so-called, preacher. Mary knew in her heart that the next morning would be her last chance for her and the girls to escape.

She hid the hunting knife she had stolen under the blanket in the lean-to, just in case Isom decided not to wait for the preacher.

During the day, while going to the creek for water, she took notice where the gate was to the corral and how it was kept shut. She also was able to locate the saddles, bridles, and canteens. If something went wrong when they made their escape attempt she didn't want to have to spend time searching for what they might need.

Isom and the younger boy went about their daily routine. Isom forked hay to the horses, sharpened an ax, stretched some hides on a rack, and replaced a worn shoe on one of his horses. The younger Isom spent most of the day chopping wood and stacking it.

Mary noticed that she was never far out of Isom's sight.

The day seemed to drag by. She found some axle grease in the barn and managed to smuggle a small handful inside the cabin. When she was sure Isom and the boy were occupied outside, she stuffed the crack on both sides of the squeaky board that had alerted Isom the previous morning.

Mary cast fleeting glimpses at the sun as it progressed slowly across the sky. In her mind she went over every detail of how she hoped it would be. *If I fail, Isom will most certainly kill us.* That thought sent chills up and down her spine. *But I'd rather we all die than allow Marilyn to be subjected to what she would face at the hands of the evil older son. I must not fail.*

Mary and Marilyn went about what they thought was expected of them. They cooked venison for supper. They found some fresh honey and decided to make hot biscuits. Mary knew men slept better on a full stomach and she wanted them to sleep sound.

After supper, to Mary's delight, Isom went to the barn and came back with a jug of home brew. She watched him turn the jug up and take a long swig time after time. *If only he would get drunk, that might make things easier,* she thought. Then suddenly a thought came that scared her to death. *What if he gets all lickered up? What if he decides not to wait for the preacher? I'll just have to cross that bridge when I come to it.*

Mary motioned to Marilyn with her head. Her daughter got the message. They led Sally toward the lean-to and pulled the blanket in place behind them. Mary placed herself nearest the door and placed the hunting knife under the fold of the blanket. She knew in her heart that she would be no match for Isom, should he come, but it was the only defense she had.

They waited on pins and needles.

They jumped at every sound, half expecting Isom to jerk the blanket aside and stumble into their room at any second. Mary clutched the knife until her knuckles ached. Her hand made sweat on the thick handle.

Finally, she heard the leather lacing of Isom's bed squeak. Soon, loud snoring rumbled from the outer room.

Marilyn and Sally drifted off to sleep. Mary lay awake, planning and praying.

Tad and Hugh watered the horses before pulling out. They didn't have long to wait after they reached the mouth of the canyon. Lupe came jogging up with his rifle in his hand and a wide smile on his face.

"We dusted a few of them didn't we?"

"Sure did," Hugh replied. "You most likely saved our bacon with that climb of yours."

"Reckon we'll run into them farther along?" Tad asked.

"Doubt it. They're most likely trying to explain to their chief how they lost so many warriors and still don't have nothing to show for it."

"Sure hope you're right."

"We best make some tracks though, just in case."

By late that afternoon Hugh figured they had crossed into Texas.

"Another couple of days and we ought to be home, boys." he told them.

That news made them ride a little faster.

They made camp that night beside a small stream and built a nice campfire. They cooked a nice supper and ate until they couldn't hold another bite. Afterward, they sipped coffee, listened to the night sounds, and thought about home.

"You gonna go back to being the Sheriff's deputy?" Tad asked.

"If he'll have me. I like Lubbock. Nice little town. Nice folks there too."

"Was you ever a lawman before you took the job with Sheriff Paxton?"

"Nope."

"You ever think about getting married again?"

"Thought about it a time or two, trouble is, most women ain't interested in a man like me, always on the move, always looking over his shoulder. What about you? You got a girl?"

"Well, kinda."

"What's her name?"

"Tad is sweet on Christine Holly," Lupe volunteered, laughing.

"Well, you are sweet on her sister, Cleo."

"Won't be long until both of you will be getting hitched."

"Not me," Lupe said. "I want to see some country first."

"You never told me that before," Tad said, shooting a look at his friend.

"That's cause I just decided."

Tad chewed on that bit of information for awhile and he didn't much like the taste of it. The thought of being separated from Lupe didn't set well. *Wonder what had gotten into Lupe? Why has he decided that he wants to leave the Littlejohn Valley?* He was still wrestling with that question as sleep overtook him.


The first grayness of the new day crept through the single window of the cabin and made its way into the lean-to.

*It's time,* Mary thought, slipping quietly from under their blanket. She took a long, shuddery breath, tried unsuccessfully to swallow back the fear that crept up her throat, and gripped the knife in her right hand.

She listened intently. The loud snoring continued from the other room. She pulled aside the blanket covering of the door and looked through. Isom and his son were both sleeping soundly.

Tip-toeing barefooted, she inched her way across the room one careful step at a time. The dim light showed her the holster and pistol lying on the floor near Isom's bed. If she could only reach it without waking him.

Her heart raced. She was afraid to breathe. *Just another few steps,* she thought. Isom coughed and turned over with his back to her.

She reached out a hand and touched the pistol. Slowly, carefully, she slid it out of the holster. She knew very little about guns. T. J. had tried to teach her how to use a pistol but she never had liked them. Could she remember now what little she had learned?

She turned the pistol so she could see inside the cylinders. It seemed to be fully loaded, the nose of five bullets showed clearly.

She took a deep breath, swallowed hard, and pulled back

the hammer. She hadn't expected the noise to be so loud. When the hammer locked in place the sound seemed deafening in the confines of the room.

Isom bolted upright.

George and his small posse were up well before first light. They didn't take time for coffee or breakfast, they were all anxious to get on the trail.

As the first grayness slipped over the mountain they were in the saddle and moving. At first Wolf-cries-in-the-night walked and led his horse. As the light improved he swung onto his mustang and their pace quickened.

The tracks followed the bank of a small mountain stream for a mile or so and then swung into a small rock strewn canyon. The canyon opened into a long, narrow valley with a stream that split the valley in half. On the bank of the stream, maybe a quarter mile away was a cabin.

George's heart leaped at the sight. The Indian tracker lifted an arm and pointed.

Mary gasped when Isom sat upright on his bunk. He swung a look. Mary lifted the pistol. She stood no more that five feet from the man. He glared at her with hatred in his eyes but made no move toward her.

Her finger was on the trigger. She wanted with all her heart to shoot this monster that had caused them so much pain. She hesitated.

She saw his gaze cut to her left. Was it a trick to divert her attention? She sensed, rather than heard, a movement. She backed up a step and cast a quick glance in the direction Isom had looked.

Carlyle had somehow awaked and saw what was happening. He reached for his pistol that lay on the floor beside his bunk. *Just pretend you are pointing your finger,* T. J. had told her. *Squeeze the trigger, don't jerk it.*

She swung the nose of the pistol and squeezed the trigger. The explosion jolted her. The younger Isom was slammed against the wall by the force of the blast.

Isom leaped from the bed. He took a long step and hurtled through the air toward Mary. Swinging the pistol and not having time to aim, she fired.

A body hit the floor at her feet. She had no idea if she had hit him or not. Then suddenly a strong hand clasped around her ankle. Without even thinking she used both thumbs to draw back the hammer again.

She looked down. Isom was lying on his back at her feet. His evil eyes stared up at her in disbelief. His lips curled into a snarl.

"I'll cut your heart—!"

His words were drowned out by the loud explosion from the pistol in her hand. As if caught in a trance, she pulled back the hammer again and again, firing point blank into the monster that lay at her feet. With each shot Isom's body shook from the impact. Finally, the pistol clicked on a spent cartridge.


A pistol shot rang out and echoed through the little valley, then another. Before the echo had died from the first shot, George had kicked his gray into a full gallop, heading for the cabin as fast as his horse could carry him.

Dread coiled inside him, twisting, turning, writhing like a snake, fear so intense it left him cold inside. What would he find in the cabin? Had Isom murdered them all? He lashed his mount with the ends of his reins, urging it to greater speed.

As he came to a sliding stop in front of the cabin with his pistol firmly in his fist, a bedraggled Mary emerged with a still smoking pistol in her hand. Her face was black and blue. She looked ravaged, blanched, and stark. Marilyn and Sally were clutched close.

Relief, overwhelming joy, and a feeling of indescribable love surged through him. He leaped from his saddle and rushed to them, gathering all three into his arms.

"Are you all right? Are you hurt?"

"We're all right now that you are here."

"What about Isom and his boys?"

"Isom's dead. So is the younger one. The one called Jubal rode out this morning, I don't know where."

"No matter, you're safe, that's all that's important to me now."

He took her in his arms and drew her close. He felt her cling to him as tightly as he was clinging to her. He held her, offering warmth, and comfort, and love.

Caleb galloped up, flew from his horse, and swept Marilyn off her feet, crushing her in his arms, both sobbing uncontrollably. Homer Green dismounted. He saw little Sally standing beside the others and realized immediately that something was terribly wrong with her. Walking over to her, he began to speak softly and soothingly to her, hugging her to his chest.

Wolf-cries-in-the-night pushed through the door of the cabin and was gone for several minutes. Finally emerging, he walked over to the Sheriff.

"He dead. He shot five times. He much dead."

# Chapter XXI

In time, her weeping ran its course. Meanwhile, George was more than content to hold her in his arms.

"Want to talk about it?" He finally asked.

"Not now, all I want is to get away from this place as quickly as possible."

"Then we'll leave right away."

True to his word, in less than half an hour they were in the saddle and headed toward home.

They made camp that night beside the little stream not far from where Mary had been dragged earlier. Their Indian tracker disappeared into the woods and came back with four large fox squirrels. Marilyn made squirrel stew for their supper.

After everyone had eaten their fill, Caleb and Marilyn walked down by the creek to talk. Homer Green had taken little Sally under his wing and was teaching her how to play mumble peg with his pocketknife. George and Mary sat beside the campfire sipping coffee and listening to the peaceful crackle of the fire and sounds of the night: The gentle gurgling of the water over rocks, the wind humming sweetly through the pine trees and the black velvet night wrapped itself around them.

"How long will it take us to get home?" Mary asked.

"Three days, more or less."

"I'm so thankful that you came. I never doubted that you would."

"You were very brave, all of you. Not many would have survived what you went through."

"I had a lot to live for. Have you heard anything from Tad and the others?"

"Not yet, but I've got a hunch they will be back soon."

"George."

He swung a look. Their eyes met. He looked deep into her blue eyes for a time, his eyes searching, his bright gaze holding hers.

"When Tad returns . . ."

She let her words trail off, unfinished, yet full of promise.


They awoke to a cold north wind. George and the Indian were tightening the cinches on their saddles, readying the horses for the day's travel. George glanced quickly at the dark clouds building over the mountains behind them to the west and then spoke over his shoulder.

"You thinking what I'm thinking?"

"Storm come. We move away from stream. Get to higher ground."

"Mary," George shouted. "Get the girls mounted. We need to get moving. Storm coming."

George, Homer, and Caleb were the only ones that had rain slickers. They gave them to the women. In less than a mile the rain hit with a fury. The wind lashed at them and drove the large raindrops at them in a solid sheet of water. They bowed their heads and kept riding.

Wolf-cries-in-the-night led the string of riders and reined his pinto up beside a rocky ledge that jutted out from a hillside. He pointed.

George, Homer, and Caleb helped the women down from their horses, and underneath the ledge. The men quickly strung a rope between two rocks and tied the horses to the line. The dugout beneath the overhang was small, but large enough for everyone to get out of the rain. They huddled together under the three rain slickers and shivered from the cold.

Minutes stretched into hours. Still the rain fell from the dark sky. Thunder rolled in from the mountains. Lightening stabbed the earth. The frightened horses whinnied and pulled at their lines.

Finally, by mid-afternoon, the rain slackened to a steady sprinkle. They decided that since they were all soaked to the skin anyway they might just as well get as far as they could toward home.

The horses plodded steadily along. The rain stopped and soon the ground that passed beneath the horses' hooves was as dry as a bone. Twilight turned to full dark and still they rode on. A full moon hung high and proud. Stars winked from a black canopy.

George watched the woman closely. They clung gamely to their saddles, but finally it was clear they could go no further.

Whistling through his teeth to Wolf-cries-in-the-night, George motioned with his arm at a twisted arroyo nearby. He swung his gray down the sloping bank. The dry gully was choked with gnarled mesquite, stunted cactus, and agave grew in scattered clumps.

"We'll rest awhile," he said, stepping stiffly to the ground.

He didn't get an argument from anyone. Within minutes they all had spread their ground sheets, crawled under their blankets and were fast asleep. All, that is, except the Indian. He sat cross-legged with a blanket around his shoulders and his rifle lying across his legs.

Wolf-cries-in-the-night had gathered wood for a fire and had coffee boiling when George opened his eyes. It was already daylight.

He rolled out from under his blanket, shook out his boots, and pulled them on. The Indian handed him a cup of steaming coffee as George squatted on his haunches near the fire. He blew the steam away and chanced a sip. It burned all the way to his stomach but tasted mighty fine.

"We get to town tomorrow," the Indian said.

"Could we make it by morning if we rode awhile tonight?"

The tracker nodded.

Mary rose from her blanket and joined them near the fire. George handed her a cup of coffee.

"Did I hear you say we could get to Lubbock by morning?"

"If we ride awhile tonight," George answered.

"Then let's do it. I'm anxious to get home."

George turned a gaze on Mary. Her dress was torn and dirty. Her hair matted, her face was still swollen and her lip had a large scab forming. It was obvious she was worn to a frazzle; still, she was the most beautiful woman he had ever seen.

After a skimpy breakfast of fried salt pork and coffee they saddled their horses for the day's long ride. The wind still had a chill to it. The Indian tracker asked each of the women for their blanket. He took his long knife and cut a hole in the center and handed them back. With motions, he showed them how to poke their heads through the holes and drape the blanket over themselves.

"Serape," he said. "Keep warm."

All day they rode, stopping only for short periods to rest the horses and water them when the opportunity presented itself. The day stretched into night and still they pushed on. Finally, it was apparent that the women could go no further. George called a halt.

"We'll rest up here and get a fresh start in the morning."

The closer Tad and his companions got to home the better they felt. Even their tired horses seemed to find a new source of strength and lengthened their strides as Lubbock came into view off in the distance.

"Shore gonna be good to get back home," Tad said.

"You just thinking about seeing Christina Holly again," Lupe kidded.

"Yeah, that too."

"I can't wait to sleep in a real bed again," Hugh told them. "Been so long I forgot what it feels like. Let's hurry these horses some."

They rode into Lubbock as the sun was settling below the western horizon. Old Silas at the livery was sitting on a bench out in front whittling and saw them coming. He put away his knife and hurried out to meet them.

"See you boys made it back all in one piece."

"Barely," Tad said, stepping down.

"Hate to be the one to have to tell you, Tad, but your mother and sisters have been kidnapped. The sheriff is on the trail now. They've been gone might near a week now."

The news hit Tad like a wagonload of bricks. His heart dropped to his boots. His stomach twisted. Fear raced through him.

"Tell me about it," Hugh Overstreet asked anxiously. "Start from the beginning and don't leave nothing out."

The old hostler told how it was. Hugh, Tad, and Lupe listened intently. When the telling was done they asked for more.

"Who's with George?" Hugh wanted to know.

"The tracker, Wolf-cries-in-the-night, Homer Green, and his son Caleb is the only ones with him. The sheriff sent the rest of the posse back, said he wouldn't be back until he found them."

"You say the one's he's after is named Isom?"

"Yep, Wiley Stubblefield found a wanted poster on them in the sheriff's office after he got back. The old man is named Amos. He had three sons fore your ma shot one of them. They're wanted all over Texas."

"Any idea where they are from?"

"Nope, got no idea."

"Well, see to our horses, will you?" Hugh told him. "We may need them come morning."

"That black stallion is some kind of horse. Where'd you come by him?"

"Belongs to Tad."

Old Silas was still admiring the stallion when they slid their rifles from the saddle boots. Tad slung his saddlebags over his left shoulder and carried his Henry rifle in his right hand as they headed toward the hotel.

"What do you think we ought to do, Mr. Hugh?" Tad asked.

"Don't rightly know, son, wouldn't do your folks any good to go traipsing off half-cocked. Let's get settled in the hotel and talk to some of the others before we decide what's best."

They checked into the hotel and arranged for separate rooms. After a hot bath, they went downstairs to the hotel café.

"I want the biggest beef steak you can find and all the trimmings," Hugh told the waitress.

"Make that two," Lupe said.

"Make it three," Tad agreed.

While they were eating Wiley Stubblefield walked in and pulled up a chair.

"Heard you were back in town, sure sorry about Mary and the girls. We were hoping to have heard something from the sheriff by now. Ray Sawyer felt like he could be of more use taking care of things out at your place instead of with the posse."

Tad just nodded and said nothing.

"Think there's any chance to pick up the trail?" Hugh asked the storekeeper.

"Not a chance. This wind has been fierce the last couple of days. It would have wiped out any tracks, nothing to do now but wait."

Tad laid down his fork and stared straight ahead. The thought of him just sitting around waiting stuck in his craw.

"I can't. My mother and sisters are out there somewhere going through no telling what. I can't just sit around and wait."

"What *can* we do, son?" Hugh asked.

"Don't rightly know, but I've got to do something. You say the sheriff headed northwest?"

"Yes, but that covers a lot of territory. We could look for a month of Sundays and not find them out there."

"Don't matter," Tad said. "Come morning I'm heading northwest."

Sunup found Tad at the livery saddling the buckskin. He lifted the cinch straps and was about to buckle it when Lupe walked up with his saddlebag slung over his shoulder and his rifle in his hand.

Without a word he draped his saddlebags across the corral fence and propped his rifle against it. He went to the stall and led his pinto out and began saddling up.

"Where you going?" Tad asked.

"With you."

Just then Hugh Overstreet strode up.

"You didn't think you were going without me, did you?"

Tad lifted one corner of his mouth in a thin grin.

They set the packsaddle on old Solomon's back and girded it in place.

"We'll need to stop by the store and stock up on trail supplies," Hugh said.

The sun was two hours old when they finished loading the pack mule. They were about to step into the saddle when a commotion at the edge of town turned their heads. Townsfolk were rushing from stores onto the boardwalk. Women were clapping their hands. Men were sending up cheers.

A single-file line of horses were strung out headed into town. Sheriff George Paxton led the way on his dappled gray. Mary was next in line, riding one of the Missouri Brown mules. Homer Green was next in line with Sally riding behind him, her small arms locked around his waist. Caleb Green and Marilyn rode side by side. Wolf-cries-in-the-night brought up the rear of the column leading two extra horses.

Tad dropped the reins to his buckskin and raced up the street to meet them as fast as his shaky legs would carry him. Mary spotted her son and slid off the mule and ran to meet him. Tad opened his arms and his mother filled them. They hugged one another and sobbed openly.


One month after their rescue and return to Lubbock, Mary Littlejohn and George Paxton were married in the church in town. Marilyn and Sally served as Maid of Honor and bridesmaid. Hugh Overstreet, the newly appointed Lubbock County Sheriff, served as best man. Tad gave his mother away and Lupe was groomsman.

Marilyn and Sally spent a week in town with Wiley and Doris

Stubblefield to give Mary and her new husband a few days alone.

Tad bought the little 'Lost Valley", as he called it, that he had fallen in love with and hunted in so many times. He built a fence across the mouth of it and hired some men from town to help him build a new cabin.

"I'm gonna find me some good brood mares and let that stallion breed some of the finest horses Texas has ever seen," he told his friend, Lupe, as they leaned on the rail fence and watched the magnificent black stallion grazing peacefully beside the stream. "Sure you won't stay and help me?"

Lupe toed a stirrup and swung up onto his pinto.

"No, I've got an itch to see the country and make my own way. I'll be back from time to time. *Adios, hasta la vista,*"

"*Vaya con Dios,* my brother."

~The End~

## *About the Author*

I was born and raised in eastern Oklahoma—formerly known as the Indian Territory. My home was only a half-day's ride by horseback from old historic Fort Smith, Arkansas, home of Judge Isaac C. Parker, who became famous as "The Hanging Judge."

As a young boy I rode the same trails once ridden by the likes of the James, Younger, and Dalton gangs. The infamous "Bandit Queen," Belle Starr's home and grave were only thirty miles from my own home. I grew up listening to stories of lawmen and outlaws.

For as long as I can remember I love to read, and the more I read the more I wanted to write. Hundreds of poems, songs, and short stories only partially satisfied my love of writing. Dozens of stories of the "old west" gathered dust on the shelves of my mind. When I retired I began to take down those stories, dust them off, and do what I had dreamed of doing ever since I was a small boy—writing historical western novels.

Dusty Rhodes love to hear from his many fans.